The Judas Syndrome

Book one in the series

Michael E. Poeltl

Michael E. Poeltl

SECOND EDITION

ISBN 978-0-9813168-0-2

To the future
May you be kind.

Michael E. Poeltl

The more rapidly a civilization progresses, the sooner it dies for
another to rise in its place.
Havelock Ellis, The Dance of Life

Michael E. Poeltl

Joel Speaks....

My name is Joel. Ever heard the expression; Shit happens? It hardly does justice to what's happened to me, but in a pinch, it will suffice as a summation of my life these past few months.

I know now that a single action can put in motion a series of repercussions. Should that action be positive, the repercussions are rewarding, but when that action is negative, so too are the events to follow. A single action can change you forever. Sometimes, the results can be disastrous if the deed is large enough, and the intent evil enough.

My friends can attest to this. My friends have always featured prominently in my life. Some helped shape my earliest memories, while others I only met in high school. But as much as my friends have shaped my past, no memories can compare to those of the last few months as we struggled to survive. Their actions changed me, and how I lived as much as mine shaped their daily lives. The rewards were bittersweet for those of us who made it out of this thing alive. We kept our lives but lost our innocence and our faith, the lack of which can empty your existence like water evaporating under a relentless sun.

And for the rest of us...

Chapter One

The apocalypse came quickly. Growing up in a small northern town over two hundred kilometers away from any major city left me impervious to global threats like war, famine, disease, and vicious dictators. I watched the news every night and knew the world wasn't right, but I never suspected just how wrong things were getting.

*****

Three weeks before disaster struck, I planned to go to the town park's beer garden. Remembering past events, I suspected there would be a few fights throughout the evening, but nothing too brutal unless some yahoos from another town decided to show up and make a play for our beer and women—lowbrow stuff. Rarely worked on the girls. I tried to avoid these free-for-alls unless a friend was getting the worst of it.

That friend was usually Sonny. As much as I loved the guy, drinking with him was a risky undertaking for me and him. Big, beefy, and fearless, he attracted idiots like flies. Frustrated by a week of shitty work for shittier pay, whiskey-fed farm boys would try to score a reputation by taking on Big Sonny. When he handed their asses to them, they'd push the strength in numbers angle and come back with some friends. That's when I had to get involved, whether I liked it or not. The morning after, it was hard to tell which hurt worse - my hangover or my bruised ribs. Wincing at past memories, I stocked up on aspirin.

My buddy Connor pulled into my driveway shortly after four-thirty that afternoon. The sky was bluer than it had been for days, and I was in the front yard, trailing my bare toes through the lawn pond. The goldfish were strangely agitated, darting for cover instead of swimming to the surface for food.

"Just got off work - thank God!" Connor had a summer job with a landscaping company, so he'd spent the day sweating under a blazing sun and listening to hovering housewives whine out instructions and warnings. "If you're done with your goldfish pedicure, let's get some beer for tonight!"

"*Beer?* What for? We're going to the gardens."

"No, *we're not*, buddy. Our plans have changed."

"What are you talking about?" I wasn't sure I liked this. I wouldn't say I liked missing the opportunity to hook up - you were as likely to stumble into a girl as a fight on a night like that.

"Listen, you like a little excitement in your life, right?"

"Sure, unless it gets me in jail or family court."

"Good, then you're in." He started to roll his window back up.

"Not so fast. Let's *assume* I'm interested. What's the new plan?"

Connor smirked. "Be ready to go at six o'clock."

"Sonny's expecting me at the gardens. He'll kill me if I don't show."

"We have the rest of our lives to pull Sonny out of the fire. He won't miss us."

*****

I had to admit that I was intrigued. If Connor was willing to forgo the beer gardens, then his plans must really be something. If not, the gardens weren't going anywhere. True to his word, he picked me up at six, and we headed off toward parts that were, for me, unknown.

At the beer store, we ran into Ruby. It was rumored that she had slept with the entire senior hockey team. Two years ago, she was Connor's girlfriend; now, she regularly came between the jocks and their straps.

Her brows arched at the sight of us. "What are you guys doing here: getting some drinks to warm up for the gardens?" She loved to answer her own questions. I let Connor field this one - I was too busy staring at how her melon-sized breasts were trying to push out of her blouse.

"No, we've got other plans. It's hush, hush, but it'll be better than trying to keep up with the fall-down drunks at the gardens."

I added, "He won't tell me either, and I'm going with him."

"Oh, well, I just thought I'd see you there. Maybe get to dance with you or whatever."

The *whatever* part had sweet possibilities. I wondered if it was too late to change my mind when Connor nudged me.

"Sorry, another night."

We bought the beer and returned to the car, where I finally yelled, "Are you going to tell me where we're headed?"

Connor smiled and motioned for me to get into the car. Once seated, he reached into his shirt pocket and pulled out two acid hits.

"We don't want to be at the beer gardens while we're on these," he grinned. While I peered closely at the stuff, Connor added, "I've only done it a couple of times before, but man, such a good time."

"You sure? I've heard bad things from people who've had a *bad time* on this stuff."

"Look, I won't lie to you; it's intense. It's not James Bong." James Bong was our pet name for his pipe. "It's a different high altogether. You see things. Funny things, though." He playfully smacks me in the arm and chuckles. "It's all good."

If anybody could make me see the lighter side of an otherwise risky situation, it was Connor. I'd done mushrooms once and enjoyed the trip, and he explained that acid was: "mushrooms times ten." I hated math in school but liked that number, so I forgave him for ruining my sex life and said, "I'm in."

Settling into my seat, I closed my eyes and let him drive.

*****

Fifteen minutes later, we were at a spot that every local pothead, underage drinker, and horny couple without a room knew all too well. It was the scenic crest of a hill that overlooked the distant city to the south and everything in between. The cops rarely came up to raid the under-agers, and Connor knew they'd all be on duty at the gardens anyway.

"The perfect place to start the summer, don't you think, old fella?" Connor, busting to drop his hit, dug into his pocket.

"Not a bad call," I allowed. As I handed him a beer from the backseat cooler, I added, "You know you should have planned this better: - no ladies up here."

"Don't be so sure I haven't taken care of you, old man." He gave me that knowing smile, and I had to grin. There might be more to this night than met the eye.

He popped his hit under his tongue and held mine out to me. "What the hell, let's party."

Five minutes passed.

"Can you feel it yet?" Connor's brain was buzzing. *Buzzzzzz.* I swear I could hear it - like an old refrigerator.

The question made me realize that I was captivated by the synthetic drug. My head reeled, and my perspective went beautifully ape shit. "B-i-n-g-o." That was all I could say.

I studied my hands for what felt like the first time in my life. There they were, irreplaceable, attached to my arms at the wrist. They were so sensitive to the touch with all their digits, movable joints, and feelings; *that's it!* Touch was born of the hand, of its fingers, my fingers; they were my own and priceless.

I spun around in slow motion, still marveling at the dexterity and beauty of my hands. Connor was lying on the ground with his mouth wide open. Watching me, he started to laugh, and I followed.

Suddenly, a voice broke my psychedelic reverie. I watched it all shatter like stained glass to make way for reality.

"Someone sounds like they're having way too much fun."

Sara and Julia were coming up the hill, each upward step making their denim skirts ride higher up their thighs. I'd known both girls for years, and when their smirks and coy greetings clued me in that they were joining us by prior arrangement, I realized that this was what Connor had meant by *taking care of me.* I could have kissed the stoned bastard, as I'd had a crush on Sara for months, but I didn't want to risk sending the wrong message to the girl I'd admired so long from a distance.

"Want a beer?" Shit. It was all I could think to say.

"Thanks, guys, don't mind if we do." Flirtier than I'd ever seen her, Sara settled on the grass beside me and took a swig from my bottle. I watched her red lips draw tight around the bottle head and thanked God that she dumped her deadbeat boyfriend two weeks ago.

Hours later, and ten beers into the night, I found Sara pushing me down, her beer-sweetened breath in my face. Beside us, I think that Connor and Julia were engaging in something similar, but I honestly did not care at that point. Sara remained my focus: her mouth, her eyes, her hands.

Chapter Two

Light brightened the eastern sky and rolled across the hilly terrain, landing hot and bright on our faces. We rose, shook the morning moisture off our clothes, dressed, and drove back into town. Sara and I took her car. Last night, she admitted she'd had a crush on me since the Christmas formal dance. We weren't sure we had anything in common, but if that department turned out to be a dud, we were sure compatible naked.

When we arrived at my place, I gave her a tour of the house and made breakfast. We were alone: Mom was still in Australia, and Kevin, who rented a room from us, was at work. After eating our fried egg sandwiches, we retired to the family room to watch TV.

The Grim Reaper was in the news again. This anonymous maniac had everyone on edge with his vows to create a better world by kyboshing the old one. He first made his presence known last May via a website that went through so many proxies that its source was indecipherable. He claimed to have acquired some thirty nuclear missiles from Iraq, employed by Saddam's secret service, smuggling them out before the small country had agreed to the lengthy UN weapons inspections. He released messages to the media threatening to inflict worldwide nuclear devastation should the various governments not heed his 'suggestions,' which included destroying schools and houses of worship, both of which he accused of turning people into automatons. No one knew who he was and whether he was serious or what, but a report had been leaked that the UN was searching for missing warheads, and that was enough to make the Grim Reaper a 24-7 news feature.

"You know, if that Grim Reaper is for real, we're pretty screwed." Sara looked uneasy.

"I think the government can deal with this chump." I put my arm around her, noticing she had gooseflesh under her blouse. She rested her head against my chest, her perfumed hair fluttering each time I exhaled. We both closed our eyes and drifted off.

*****

When I awoke, it was four-thirty in the afternoon. Sara was gone but had left a note on the coffee table asking me to call her later. I smiled and made a mental note to thank Connor when I saw him again.

The house was too silent, so I turned on the radio. The news was on, but instead of another Grim Reaper broadcast, they were airing an investigative report on a new drug that had proven over eighty-five percent effective in treating depression. I laughed and swigged some orange juice. A drug like that would go over big time in the face of the world's current problems. Shit, they should dump it in water supplies everywhere. Then, if the Grim Reaper struck, we would fry happy.

A sudden crash of thunder overhead drowned out the commentator's voice. Grinning in anticipation, I ran to the front door, opened it, and stepped onto the porch. The skies were the color of slate, creating an unreal backdrop for the vibrant green trees and hills. I wasn't sure what I loved the most about thunderstorms: the unearthly stillness that preceded them, the glorious shout of thunder, or the freaky light show in the sky. I was still pondering the issue when my housemate Kevin pulled into the driveway.

"Joel!" he shouted as he vaulted out of his pickup. "It's going to storm-close the windows in the addition before my paintings get soaked!"

Before I could react, the skies opened up. Kevin was drenched before he reached the front door. He tore past me, running up the stairs three at a time. I heard the frantic sound of windows slamming. Then he came back down; his glasses dotted with rain and 'Pro Painters' t-shirt clinging to his bony frame.

"Shit. That was close. I need a drink." He reached into one of his deep pockets. "I brought some whiskey with me. Do we have any ginger ale left?"

"Yeah, there should be some in the fridge. Make me one, too. I'll be there in a minute."

Thin and pasty white, Kevin was often asked whether he was sick. Amused by the attention, he played up to his audience by wearing tight clothes, slicking back his thick brown hair, and sporting black-framed glasses. A calculated attempt to give himself the classic heroin-chic, starving - yet successful- artist aura.

The studio above the three-car garage also doubled as his bedroom; he'd arranged to rent the space from my mom while she was away. It was perfect timing: if she'd been home, his all-night binges at the easel would have worsened her insomnia and eventually left him homeless.

*****

That night, Sara came over. She told me she was sleeping over. I liked how forward she was with me. It complimented my more withdrawn personality. Before bed, I introduced her to a ritual I'd always cherished.

I guided her onto the overhang just outside my bedroom window. The storm long passed; the night sky was beset with stars. Pointing upward, I asked her to pick a point of light and stay with it. Then, standing up, I eased Sara to her feet and whispered, "Have you ever stood stargazing and felt the earth move under your feet?"

I showed her something I'd discovered one starry night many years ago. I'd been leaning against a pine tree in the woods behind the house, gazing at all the famous constellations: Big Dipper, Orion, and others. Suddenly, I felt like I was moving, although my feet had not budged. I quickly learned that the sensation was the earth's rotation, something the average person did not notice until the stars provided a reference point. A smile came to Sara's face as she experienced the same feeling now in my arms. Connected.

*****

After breakfast, Sara helped me study, bouncing questions off one another. The coming week meant exams for everyone and the commencement of summer jobs for most. I will start working in another three weeks. I'd explained to the interviewer that my exams ended then when, in fact, school would be finished in one week. I just wanted the extra fourteen days to relax, party, and have no commitment to anything except fun.

Little did I know that my summer job would be the very least of my inconveniences two weeks from now.

Chapter Three

The Grim Reaper was mentioned on the radio again. I listened to the broadcast while shaving. Hostess Samantha McGinnis was grilling some military figurehead about the magnitude of the Reaper threat. The guest assured her that the media had taken another psycho's threats and blown them out of proportion to increase their ratings.

"There is no possibility of anything coming of this." he said calmly. "No single individual has the resources to pull off an operation as large as he's suggesting. It is absurd to believe so and unfortunate that this man can instill such fear into so many via a tool like the Internet."

I changed the channel and started dinner. Moments later, Connor breezed through the front door with a box of beer in hand.

"I've got a great idea for our last weekend before you start working!"

I popped the case open and helped myself to a beer. "Let's hear it."

"Let's get everyone together, I mean *everybody*, and go up to the lake for a couple of days. Camping, canoeing, a little fishing. We'll go to the same spot we did with Ruby and Jill two years ago." He stopped to grab a drink. "Only it'll be way better this time. Get Sara and Julia to come, you know?"

It sounded good, but Sonny appeared behind Connor before I could say so. Both of us jumped at the sight of him.

"Shit! Sonny!" I complained. "Can't you knock once in a while?"

He didn't answer. Face grim, he grabbed a beer from Connor's pack but didn't open it. He flexed his fingers like the beer can was a neck he longed to break. "Someone's been picking the bud off our plants. Any ideas who?"

"What happened?" This was upsetting as the plants should be ready to harvest in another week. We'd cultivated twenty marijuana plants along the farmers' field the length of my property line.

"Half the crop is missing. That's a lot of weed! Pisses me off." He opened the beer can, took an enormous swallow, and sat down. "Well, I have to hurt somebody over this." He paused and then brightened. "Hey, I hear you and Sara from Cedar Valley hooked up!"

When I nodded, he winked and turned to Connor. "And what are you doing with a girl like Julia, Connor? She's not your type."

"Maybe we're coming up in the world. You should try it."

"Bite me. After Ruby, dating a cow would be coming up in the world."

He had a point. We all chuckled and clinked cans. Then Connor said, "Sonny, what do you say about camping at the lake next weekend?"

He shrugged his massive shoulders, pushing in the tab on another beer. "Yeah, sounds like a plan."

"Help yourself, by the way." Connor winks, and Sonny shows a toothy grin.

Our buddy Earl joined us an hour later. Earl was the human equivalent of a dynamite stick: light his fuse, and disaster would follow. He always wore a baseball cap jammed over his shaggy ginger mop and was a gun nut, which wasn't a good match for his temperament. But that evening, I was happy to see him come in with his rifle slung across his shoulders. Maybe he would finally shoot that damn skunk.

*****

I'd first encountered the skunk almost two weeks earlier. Earl and I spent the afternoon cruising along the forest trails on Dad's five-wheeler. I was driving. Earl saw the skunk first, planted firmly in the path ahead. He yelled for me to stop, and I did, but the sudden motion sent him flying off the vehicle. He landed on his shoulder and rolled into the little black-and-white bastard, who did what all skunks do when they're pissed off. I remembered Earl's 22, which we'd brought along for target practice, and threw it to him, backing the five-wheeler up frantically as the stench became intolerable. Before Earl could even aim, the skunk, missing its left front foot, hobbled off into the bushes that lined the trail. I'd seen it on my property ever since: on the front lawn, beside the pool, in the garage.

It seemed to stare at me with those beady black eyes. Perhaps I imagined this. Either way, it made me nervous. Though I had been prone to panic attacks since my father's untimely death, I couldn't explain why this *skunk* played on my anxieties.

*****

Earl was soaking wet and annoyed as he entered the kitchen. "I can't shoot a skunk in this shit!" He gestured toward the window, streaked with rain. The weather had taken a turn during dinner.

"You can't shoot a skunk at all!" Sonny reminded him. We laughed.

"Nice, Sonny, thanks." Earl laid the rifle carefully against the wall and peeled off his wet shirt and jacket. "Well, if I see that little prick here tonight, Stinky will realize that all skunks don't go to Heaven." A sinister, anticipatory grin replaced his scowl.

"Here, Earl, light this for us." Connor passed him a freshly rolled joint. We smoked it and retired to the addition. Surrounded by Kevin's art, we sat and listened to the rain crashing on the roof. This was an absolute monster storm. We were safe, though; we reveled in storms such as these. I felt safe in my father's house.

*****

Earl was up first on Saturday morning, being the resilient party animal he was, so he answered it when the doorbell rang.

Jake Sanders was sitting on the stoop. Jake was the sort that just showed up at parties, the kind of guy you saw occasionally, which was good considering we could only take him in short spurts. Jake was a casebook addict, strung out on my doorstep and looking for a hit. I was willing to bet that he was the one who stole our bud, though I would never have told Sonny that. Jake used to be one of us, one of our best friends. Then he began chasing the dragon, and now he just ate, slept, and did drugs.

His mother had been killed along with my father on the way home from their shared business venture in the neighboring town. Our families were partners in a hardware store. Maybe that was why I felt I should try to understand and help him instead of turning my back as so many others had. His dad turned to the bottle after the accident, so there wasn't much support at home.

I had come downstairs in response to the doorbell and invited him in for coffee. When he entered the kitchen, Sonny stared him down as if sharing my suspicions about the theft.

"Drink this, Jake," I said as I poured a glass of O.J. "We were just going to shoot a skunk that's been hanging around here. Want to join us?"

"Can I just stick around here?"

"Sure, I'll hang back with you." Although too ashamed to admit it, I worried he might steal something to feed his habit. I waved the rest of them off to hunt the elusive skunk.

When Sonny, Earl, and Connor walked out the back door with loaded rifles, I poured Jake a coffee and asked, "Want something to eat?"

He nodded, so I started cracking eggs into a bowl. Scrambled was my specialty.

"They won't be good like Connor's, but I'll do my best." I forced a smile. Jake was my age, but I felt like I was babysitting a three-year-old.

Kevin came in while I was stirring the eggs. He was struggling with a massive board. "I'm taking it upstairs for a painting." He explained.

"That's cool. Come back down for breakfast."

"Will do!" He ascended the stairs carefully, the board wobbling in his grasp. "I brought my dog- she's just outside."

Hearing that, I ran out to the balcony and warned Earl and the guys that Kevin's dog was loose. She wasn't black and white but could rattle a bush or two, and accidents happen. They gave me the thumbs up before disappearing into the woods.

Jake ate only a few bites of breakfast and spent the rest of his visit smoking. I was relieved when he wandered off around 3 o'clock, leaving me alone with Sara and Julia, who'd dropped by for a swim and a drink. The hunting party returned to home base after 4:00 p.m. Earl was pissed that they couldn't find Stinky. I hoped that Dali, Kevin's dog, wasn't more successful in that department. We debated whether or not we should risk a barbecue under the darkening skies when the rain started.

"Again, with the rain!" Julia complained. "Damn it; history had better not be repeating itself." Last summer had been a complete washout, with over twenty-eight days of rain. The ducks had been happy, but we humans had to deal with flooded roads and basements. Cursing, Julia took Connor's arm, and they hurried inside.

Sonny pulled his van keys out of his pocket. "Alright, I'm hitting the road. I have a lot of crap to take care of at home. See you guys in a bit." He placed the *Trucker* magazine he had been reading over his head and jogged to the front of the house.

"I'm out of here too." Earl ran after him. "Call you later, Joel."

I waved goodbye, then turned to Sara, who had just climbed out of the pool. "Coming in?"

She sent me a frown. "I thought you loved staying out in a storm. Let's stick it out for a while. Could be killer, didn't you think?"

Man was this girl for me. I wished that we weren't going separate ways come the fall. God, I was pathetic, already with the separation anxiety.

We walked down where the lawn met the wild, rolling field and lay on the thick grass. The rain intensified, and thunder boomed, driving Sara`s arms around me. We remained open to the elements until the cold became too much. Springing to our feet, we raced each other into the house, where we towel-dried our hair and threw bathrobes over our swimming gear.

Connor and Julia were lounging on the living room sofa, munching sandwiches. The news was on, and as usual, it was ominous. Sara shifted uncomfortably beside me as the Grim Reaper took center stage again. Before I could reassure her, the phone rang. It was my mom, calling from Australia.

Everyone down under was as obsessed with the Reaper as we were. Mom asked if I was holding up okay. She also wondered if I needed her to come home early. I told her I wasn't bothered and that I'd rather she enjoyed her well-deserved vacation. We discussed my exams and college applications. I explained that report cards hadn't come in yet and I'd cut the grass tomorrow.

"Well, you have my number here, Joel. Call me when you have a minute. I love to hear from you. Love you."

"Bye, Mom. Have fun, okay? Love you too. Bye."

I hung up. An eerie feeling overwhelmed me.

"What is it, man?" Connor called. "Is everything alright with your mom?"

"Yeah, she just got a little spooked about that Reaper asshole." I pointed at the television. The most recent post from his website scrolled across the bottom of the screen. "Wondering if she should come home."

My heart sank. I was suddenly nauseous, and I didn't know why.

Chapter Four

Sunday came and went. I wrote my first exam on Monday and four more on Tuesday, Wednesday, and Thursday. Thanks to Sara's coaching, I thought that I did pretty well. My world seemed a perfect one, outwardly, at least. Inside, my mind periodically raced with the anxiety the Reaper had instilled in me, in all of us. I hated him for that.

My chief concern was for my mom. I just wanted her to enjoy herself. Managing Dad's business had worn her out, especially with Jake's dad continually screwing things up. At least she could relax with Connor's older brother running the place while she was gone. He was a godsend. That was what she called him.

Mom missed Dad terribly - that was why I liked her to get away from it all once a year and live. But now this asshole Reaper was messing that up. God, I hoped that they would catch him soon. It would be awful if he really had the means to carry out his threats. Maybe that was why the government didn't appear too concerned with him; perhaps his claims were so ridiculous they couldn't possibly come to pass. That was a comforting thought.

On Wednesday afternoon, I took my mother's car into town. I thought I might as well pick up what groceries I could for the camping weekend and save us from subsisting on the overpriced chips and hot dogs the more remote stores sold. When I returned home, rain began dotting my windshield. *Again!* "Why doesn't it let up already?"

I rolled down my window and yelled up to the addition. "Hey, Kev, get out here and help me unload the car." I saw his face pressed against the rain-streaked glass, followed by a thumbs-up.

With everything put away, Kevin led me into the addition to study his newest piece. He wasn't happy with it. He was into what he called his *Dark Period* that began in school, and even after being accepted at the finest Art College around, he couldn't shake the dire imagery.

"If you're having trouble coming up with disturbing shit to paint, get inside my dreams."

A twisted smile crossed his lips. "Do tell." So, I told him, and predictably, he was taken by the imagery. "Would you mind if I used those?"

"Sure. You can copyright them for all I care."

I left Kevin frantically sketching in his book and went to the backyard to cut the grass as the rain had tapered off. As I started the riding mower, I saw the three-legged skunk standing only thirty feet from me, staring, nothing but an unmown lawn between us.

"O-kay," I said aloud. Stinky broke his stare and began hopping toward me. *Jesus-* was that thing rabid? I threw the mower into high gear, turned, and fled. Glancing over my shoulder, I saw Stinky gaining on me. Suddenly, the mower stalled. I jumped off, slipped in the wet grass, and fell on my face. It was just like something out of a bad horror movie. I looked back, and there he was, right beside me. Now I was sweating. What the hell was I supposed to do?

Next, Kevin's dog barked from the house. Stinky looked up and bolted. Grateful for Dali's timing, I scrambled to my feet and ran into the house, making a beeline for the liquor cabinet and pouring myself a stiff drink.

"Do I smell a skunk?" Kevin came into the kitchen.

"What!" I lifted my wrist to my nose and sniffed. I didn't remember getting sprayed.

"Not you! The beer. Here, smell it. I think it's past its prime."

I took the bottle from him and inhaled. "Yikes! Yeah, that's nasty! You must have gotten a bad bottle." I take a shot of whiskey. "I just ran into old Stinky outside. He almost got me. I swear I'm having nightmares about that thing."

"Speaking of your nightmares, I have a rough done for you to see. Come on up."

That should be interesting. We went upstairs and into the addition, where Kevin handed me his sketchbook. Flipping through it, I suddenly stopped cold. On the page in pen and ink, there was a scene I'd been seeing in my dreams for almost a month.

A cross stood alone on desert terrain. The moon cast a long red shadow of the cross. The shadow resembled a red carpet, which rolled off the edge of a cliff into a raging fire. My face darkened. Kevin, who must have assumed I didn't like it, asked if I was okay.

"Yeah, yeah, I'm fine. Kev, this is phenomenal. It's *exactly* what I've been dreaming."

"Thanks, man. I'm going to stretch a canvas for it. I call it: *The Path to Hell is paved with Good Intentions.*"

"Perfect." I breathed deeply and willed myself to relax as I sensed a panic attack on the horizon. "I don't know what's wrong with me. Everything seems to be freaking me out lately. I'll lie down for a bit and see if that helps."

I left the addition, shaking my arms to release the anxiety creeping into my chest, leaving Kevin with more questions than answers.

My bedroom had always been a refuge for me. After closing the door, I approached my oldest friend, who watched me from his post on my desk. Rex was not a person or even a pet. My long-time confidant, who knew me better than my mom and Connor, was a Popsicle-stick Tyrannosaurus Rex.

I made him at summer camp when I was six. He stood a foot high, was painted green, and represented my proudest childhood achievement. If Rex could've talked, he would have spoken volumes about my life, but he couldn't, so I told him everything. You can't trust your closest friend with secrets. That's what my dad used to say. He knew how much I loved my dinosaur, so he urged me to use Rex as a sounding board whenever I needed to express my deepest thoughts or sweep out my darkest corners. "He'll never question or judge you," Dad said. Talking to Rex would be akin to holding a conversation with your conscience, with yourself. I didn't grasp the concept then, but Dad knew it would sink in later.

Sitting on my couch, I looked Rex in the eyes, eyes I had chosen to color a bright, piercing red. I took a deep, concentrated breath.

"Something's going on with me. The Reaper – the skunk, I'm on edge."

I picked Rex up and bounced him nervously on my lap.

"My nightmares – they started the day I heard about the Reaper. It's gotta be bullshit. But I can't shake this feeling."

Just as I finished my thought, Connor walked in.

"Joel? Hm. Talking to yourself? Freak! Just stopped in to grab my bag. I'm crashing at home tonight."

"I'll walk you out." I glanced at the clock on the wall as we descended the staircase. It was only 7:30 p.m., but I was exhausted. After seeing Connor off, I returned to my room, saluted Rex, and collapsed onto my waterbed, the water sloshing around me. The bed had seemed like a good idea when I was twelve. Now it was just a noisy, nauseating pain in the ass.

Kevin peeked in. When he saw me stretched out, his brow furrowed. "Joel, it's only seven-thirty. Are you crashing now?"

"I thought I might try an early night. Today's been a long day."

"Okay, I'm off to paint."

Later, I could hear music through the walls, something instrumental, a beautiful lullaby. Kevin took much of his inspiration from music. Said it helped him create. I liked it.

*****

I spent most of Thursday preparing for our camping weekend and involuntarily listening to the Grim Reaper updates. The media loved this guy because he was such a rating booster. The more scared people got, the more they hovered around the television and radio.

The latest news was that he had a following of religious crazies who agreed it was time for the planet to be "cleansed." These followers called themselves the Church of the Four Horsemen. The four horsemen of the apocalypse, no doubt. I agree that the world was a ruthless place where money and self-interest took priority over everything, but it had been that way since the dawn of civilization. The only way to change things would be to rip humanity up by the roots and plant new seeds, so to speak. I didn't see how it was possible unless…

Later, in the garage, while polishing Dad's car, a practice I'd observed every spring/summer since his death, my music was interrupted by more Reaper madness. "This just in off the Reaper's web page, and I quote," The announcer declared. "Money is not the root of all evil. Possessions are. We, as a society, strive to have more of everything. More than our neighbors, our brothers, and sisters. Money buys us these possessions; if we do not have the funds to purchase these material things, greed pushes us to steal. In many instances, one man will kill another to possess that which he does not have." She stopped. "I don't know about our listeners, but that hits home. A couple in my building had a break-in yesterday and were robbed and beaten." She pauses. "Is anyone else out there starting to like this guy?" It's an unpopular thought.

I shook my head as I resumed polishing. "Sounds like the Church of The Four Horsemen just signed up another member."

When commercials started out-numbering music, I tried other stations, but half the time, I'd just catch another news broadcast about that shadowy son of a bitch. Speculation abounded about the Reaper's identity. One theory was that he was not a single individual but a façade the Chinese or North Koreans created to draw attention and accusation away from themselves when they commenced nuclear warfare. Others thought he might be the Internet face of a group of Jihadists. Who would know before it was too late? I switched to my MP3 player and ignored the news.

Chapter Five

It was now Friday morning, and my duties concerning the weekend were complete. All that remained was to wait for Connor and the girls. The rest of the crew would meet us up at the lake that night.

I had about four hours to kill before they arrived in Connor's SUV, so I decided to lounge at the pool, escaping any more media on the Reaper's comings and goings. The day couldn't have been more perfect. The sky was an intense blue, like the water. A soft breeze fluttered through the forest. My palm stroked the grass as I sat cross-legged on the lawn. My anxiety diminished.

Connor and the ladies arrived right on time.

"Ready to roll, Joel?" Julia sat on the diving board and splashed her feet in the water.

"Just say when."

"I loaded all the stuff you had in the front hall into the back of the truck, buddy," said Connor. "Beer in the fridge?"

"Uh, yeah, it's in the basement fridge. There wasn't enough room in the kitchen." I closed my arms around a smiling Sara and kissed her.

"You ready to go, lover?" She grinned.

"I'm ready if you are." I stared into her beautiful green eyes, set above high cheekbones, a strong yet petite nose, and full lips.

"Oh, I'm ready." She answered. She turned towards the truck, but I caught her hand and spun her back to me. She let herself fall into me.

"You'll never want to leave. Nobody ever does."

"Then maybe we never will."

Once Connor's truck was loaded, we paused, soaked in the sunlight, faces angled upwards, eyes closed as if in silent prayer. Then we were on our way.

I settled into the front passenger seat. Just as we were backing up, I glanced toward the side of the house and saw the three-legged skunk. He was staring at me, singling me out as if to say: I'll see you when you return. I'll be here, waiting. It almost made me sick, literally. I turned to Connor. "Let's get the hell outta here."

"I hear that old man. I hear that." He backed out and took the corner just a little tighter than usual, and I left the skunk and the Reaper and thoughts of report cards behind me in a cloud of dust. I'd deal with all that later.

*****

The drive seemed longer than I remembered, but I willed myself to be patient. Soon, we'd set up camp and open our first pints around the lake. The thought made me smile with anticipation. God, how I needed to get away.

Finally, we approached the hallowed spot. The lake glistened as the moon rose and the sun was put to bed. Trees surrounded us: we passed one I knew bore mine and Jill's initials. Jill had been a sweet girl, but Jesus, what a temper! And jealous! She blamed our breakup on another girl. Of course, she did - she never considered that her attitude might have been the issue.

Connor found the perfect parking spot in a clearing, and we eagerly hopped out. The full moon illuminated our way as we ran to the lake's edge. Pines towered above us, leaning precariously over the water, their roots gripping rock as they dipped their branches into the lake. The air smelled of fresh dirt and sweet pine, and all was still and quiet save the loons calling in the distance. Stopping where the water met land, we stood and silently reflected.

"This is the place!" Connor finally shouted at the top of his lungs; arms stretched out as if to pull it all in. A smiling Julia joined him and rested her head against his shoulder.

I took Sara's hand and walked the last few feet to the stony beach. Reaching down, I cupped the water and splashed it on my face. "Refreshing!" I straightened and turned in time to catch Sarah lunging to push me in. I chuckled and caught her wrists.

"You want to play that game?" I laughed. Picking her up was easy, as she couldn't weigh more than 110 pounds, but she was feisty and nearly kicked out of my arms twice. She sent us both tumbling into the water in a third and final attempt to break loose.

"COLD!" She shrieked as she splashed for shore. I dragged her back in and ran. Laughing and coughing, I stripped to my boxers and tossed my wet clothes onto the rocks. Sara followed suit, dropping her outer garments on top of mine. God, she was a vision. I tried not to look too impressed. "Don't stop on my account." I teased as I threw her a towel.

Connor and Julia had unpacked the tents and begun setting up a few feet from his rear bumper. Sara and I hopped into the truck to change. I offered to dig the fire pit while Sara collected rocks to rim it when we emerged in dry clothes.

I used Connor's army shovel to dig. He was in love with army stuff. All his wilderness gear was from a used surplus store in town, so he liked to brag that everything he owned had seen 'action' at least once.

The shovel's story should have started here, at this spot, where so many new stories would begin, stories of struggle, horror, and survival: stories of war.

*****

The evening cooled down quickly enough to warrant starting a fire before the others showed up. Seated on our blankets, we shut off the radio and tuned into nature's unique brand of acoustics. I revealed a four-paper joint I'd rolled on the way up.

Connor put out his hand. "I'll light that bad boy up for you."

I handed the blunt to my friend and tossed him my lighter. The buck was passed around our small semi-circle several times before it had to be put out.

An hour passed. Then, we heard vehicles laboring through the last stretch of road. Connor and I staggered to our feet and ran to greet the new arrivals. I broke open one of our flares and waved it. Horns went off in response, and everyone rolled down their windows as if on cue. Like a chorus, our friends broke into excited war cries. They parked beside us and joined the party, camping gear in one hand and bottles in the other.

All the tents were erected around the crackling fire, which offered us light, warmth, and, of course, the means to cook, which came in handy once the munchies had taken hold. Hot dogs, popcorn, sausages, and toast were prepared; someone even cooked eggs and bacon. Fire meant life, but it had to be respected: it was a force and an unpredictable one. I knew how quickly something good could turn bad.

Wincing, I shook my head to derail such thoughts. Why be so morbid? I was with a solid group: many of us had been friends since the sandbox. All were the best kind of people, the type you'd want to spend your last days on earth with.

Kevin showed up at ten, and with him was someone wildly unexpected. Uninvited was a better word, and for a good reason: no one wanted to babysit a drug fiend during one of the best party weekends of the summer.

Jake.

Kevin explained sheepishly that he'd felt bad for the guy. "He was just sitting on your front porch, wondering where you had gone when I was leaving. I would have lied, but he looked so pathetic I panicked and figured *what's the difference*, and invited him to come up with me. I had no passengers, so I thought it might be nice to have a little company, but the guy slept the whole way here!"

I laughed, took him by the shoulders, and shook him playfully. "What were you *thinking*, man? Connor! Could you fix Kev a drink? He's had a long drive." A wave sent Kevin hurrying gratefully toward him.

Sonny arrived a little later with Tom and Sidney. Tom was a good guy. Not much to look at, or so the girls told us, but a stand-up person, pale, thin, with ears that stuck out a little too far. A shy kid, Tom made you feel awkward in a one-on-one situation. He and Sonny got along well, though. We figured Sonny liked having someone to protect, and guys like Tom seemed to attract bullies. Suffice it to say, once this unlikely friendship took off, no one in our school had the balls to insult Tom to his face, knowing full well they would incur Sonny's wrath.

"Hey, Joel." Sidney approached a handsome, light-skinned African American with a bulldog build and an infectious smile. He returned from England two days ago after participating in an exchange program. The 'bloke' our school got in return was cool, and the ladies loved the accent, but we missed having Sid around last semester.

I slapped him on the shoulder and helped myself to a pint from Sonny's cooler. We spent several minutes comparing the finer points of foreign women. Then nature called, so I excused myself and headed for the woods. I was still bleary-eyed, so unbeknownst to me, I walked through the fire's smoldering edge, emerging with a lit shoe. Not noticing the small flame burning a hole in the toes, I continued to the edge of the trees to relieve myself. Ten seconds into a good piss, I finally saw what had

29

onlookers in hysterics and kicked the shoe off before putting the fire out with what remained in my bladder. Honestly, that's the last thing I remember of that night.

*****

The group began to surface early the next morning, cooked out of their nylon ovens by the day's heat. John and Caroline emerged first, toweling the sweat from their brows. They had been a couple since the ninth grade and were straight shooters: they rarely drank - never mind smoked bud. Caroline was a classic beauty. Blonde, blue-eyed, and the high school's head cheerleader. John was 6' 2" and solidly built. He was one of those rare youths who knew precisely what he wanted from life and went about getting it without hesitation. Find the hot girlfriend, *check*, manage his credits and courses to become an A student, *check*, enter University, and become an architect - unfortunately, like the rest of us, his final aspiration in this line of goals would remain unchecked.

Next were Gil and Seth: these two were inseparable on weekends. All they did was fish. Between them, they'd bought a canoe for the express purpose of fishing.

Seth had come to our school late in our second last year. His family had moved from the boroughs that bordered the city to the south. Right out of the gate, it was obvious that Seth wasn't straight, and once Gil had befriended him, the mystery of Gil's sexual leanings was put to bed.

Gay or straight, we couldn't care less, but the subject had come up. Gil suffered a terrible beating last year over it, and when Sonny found out, Gil's assailant was hospitalized for three weeks. I approved wholeheartedly of vigilante justice: high school is tough enough without having to dodge hate crimes.

Freddy had been up earlier than anyone, riding his mountain bike through the endless trails and old logging roads. Binge and purge: that was his motto. Freddy was our star athlete heading to an Ivy League school on a Track and Field scholarship in the fall. He did everything to the best of his ability, usually better than most.

Connor crawled out of his personal hothouse with Julia behind him. "Set me up." he said, pointing a shaky finger at the frosty pints in our hands. "That tent's a hotbox in the morning."

Before we could continue our conversation, we heard Earl's truck roaring toward us. We knew it was Earl: his truck was as distinctive as he was. Sounded like he was still in third gear, not exactly recommended at this point in the drive, but Earl was a bit of a speed freak.

He stopped short of the campsite, spilling dirt over everything and everyone. The girls were furious, and with good reason, as they were just in transit with what might have been breakfast. As Earl jumped down from the lifted truck, we applauded his successful negotiation of the dirt roads, and he took a well-deserved bow.

I guessed that the noise of Earl's arrival woke Jake. Either that or the blistering sun. He dragged himself out of Kevin's car, where he had spent the night passed out across the back seat and joined the circular feeding frenzy. Sara set him up with a burger and orange juice.

"Forget the O.J." I snagged him a beer. "Take this, Jake."

He perked up a little and accepted the gift. Others eyeballed me, silently reminding me that Jake was an addict and that giving him alcohol might create problems later in the day.

"Thanks, Joel." He cracked it open. "I owe you one. I've got lots of pot and shrooms on me- you guys can dig into my stash." He took a shaky sip of the beer and focused on the ground, declining to look at or talk to anyone but me. Jake knew he was unwelcome here. God, I felt terrible for him. I hated that he had become this person.

After lunch, I grabbed the inflatable from the back of Earl's truck. He insisted on being the co-pilot. We took five minutes to pump it up and loaded a few beers into his backpack.

"I want to make it to the little island, set up there for a while, and smoke a big fat joint," I said.

"Hell of an idea, Joel," Earl replied. "It's good to go."

We carried our gear to the lake. After waving to the remaining group at the fire, Earl and I tossed the dingy into the water, put our bag in, and pushed out into deep water before hopping in. We each picked up a paddle and headed for the island Connor, and I had christened on our last trip.

The weather was perfect for the first twenty minutes of our voyage. However, northern storms tend to blow in quickly and violently, and the one we were about to face did just that.

Earl enjoyed the odd cigarette when under the influence and pulled out a pack he'd bought especially for the weekend. I told him to wait until we'd made it to the island. He became somewhat ornery and threatened to stop paddling until I handed him a light.

"Earl shut up and paddle the damn boat to shore!" Now I was getting pissed. Rain was starting to fall, and we were far from any land. Earl was drunk, so debate and logic were lost on him. If he were ignoring the approaching storm, he wouldn't listen to me. Next came the white caps, and I began to worry.

"Alright, you moron, here." I passed him my lighter. "Light that thing and start paddling."

Too late: our dingy veered perilously to the right, and without Earl countering my paddling, a wave hit us hard on the side and tossed the boat over in seconds. Our beer, his cigarettes, and my joint vanished beneath the choppy surface. We swam the remainder of the way to the island, towing the boat behind us, and made it to the rocky shore just as the rain really started to fall. Finding shelter under a tree, I quickly assessed our position.

"What the hell are we doing under a tree in a storm? Let's get in the open and pull the dingy over us." Now I was yelling: the thunder crashes were on top of us. We sat out the weather with the rubber boat firmly held over our heads.

"If that damn smoke didn't mean so much to you, we'd have been set."

A sudden shiver overtook him. "Could be worse." He said unapologetically.

"We could've drowned, you asshole." I wasn't going to let him off too easily. We'd both lost any trace of our former buzz, and a whole morning and a good portion of the afternoon was lost thanks to our nautical disaster.

It was an excellent gale, though. Of course, this was not how I liked approaching a storm of this magnitude, but I enjoyed it. Thunder crashed overhead again, and I yelled, "Is that all you got?"

Mother Nature answered immediately. The sky opened up and sent down great balls of water the size of marbles. The downpour lasted all of fifteen minutes. When the big black cloud trailed off into the distance, we crawled out from under the dinghy, peeled off our soaked shirts, and began exploring. As fate would have it, Gil and Seth were on the other side of the island. They'd tied the canoe to a pair of trees to keep them dry as they rode out the storm.

"You guys were over there?" Seth asked, popping open his cooler and handing us some beers. The island wasn't large, but the trees and brush in the middle were dense enough to have hidden us from one other.

"Yes, freezing our bags off." Added Earl. We took the drinks and sat down. "Gil, you got a cigarette for me?"

Gil handed him a butt from his plastic bag - what a Boy Scout. We sat for a while, watching them fish as the sun reemerged, warming our skin and soothing my temper. Seth had caught two fish already, one perch and one largemouth bass. They are an impressive pair.

"If we catch a few more, we'll feed the whole crew tonight." Declared Seth.

We fished for another hour, as Gil had two extra rods to lend. I never caught a damn thing, but Earl rivaled Seth's talent for the hunt. The day was back on track: we were well into our fourth beer, and the sun had burned away what precipitation remained on our rocky shores.

"Joel, grab the net!" Gil cried.

I leaped into action when Seth dropped Earl's catch into the bucket and handed me the net. I ventured into the water up to my knees to get some leverage on the approaching fish.

"Can you see it? As soon as you do, scoop him up. It's a big one!" Gil was leaning his full weight into the struggle, the rod reflecting the arch in his back.

"I see him now, Gil, reel him in a little more."

The fin was showing, and the tail began to whip back and forth violently just above the surface. Suddenly, the fish hurled itself out of the water and headed for Gil's face. Flinching, he dropped the rod and raised his hands to protect himself from the sharp fins. The fish sailed past him, landed in the water just beyond a large boulder, and continued swimming with the hook firmly in its mouth. The rod was hung up on some foliage. Gil reached over to cut the line with his Swiss army knife.

"It was the right thing to do," I declared, landing a hand on his shoulder. "That fish fought the good fight; I'd have let him go too."

Gil peered over his shoulder at me. "Hey, I just didn't want to lose any more line." He smiled, and we started laughing. I knew why he did it: we all did.

The lake was calm again, offering a smooth paddle to the mainland. Earl sat in the mid-section of Gil and Seth's canoe as I lay in the dingy being towed behind them, hands clasped behind my head and staring up at the warm blue sky as I wondered whether life would always be this perfect.

Chapter Six

B ack at the camp, everyone was relieved to see us. Gil and Seth skinned the fish on a large, flat rock slab a few feet from the fire. Blood ran off the stone and was swallowed up by a thirsty earth below as though we were appeasing an angry god. Shirtless and huddled around the stone, wielding knives like ancient priests at a sacrificial altar, Gil and Seth seemed to transform before me. Suddenly, they were wearing feathered headdresses and loincloths and had painted faces. I turned away, blaming the vision on whatever we'd smoked once back on the mainland, and began stoking the flames and preparing the pans.

As dusk set in, the conversation around the fire progressed from mellow dinner talk to a confrontation between Earl and Caroline over world issues. Caroline disagreed with him on the necessity of war as the great leveler. Practically every time we had a weekend away, Earl got into a debate with someone on this subject.

"Earl," I said, "we're not on this again, are we?"

He smirked, took a sip from his pint, and kept up the discussion with Caroline.

"Do you think this'll lead into his infamous end-of-the-world speech?" I asked Connor.

"Is the pope Catholic?"

It didn't take Earl long to find the opening he'd been waiting for. Caroline said, "You actually believe we need world wars, famine, and disease? You think we *need* things that extinguish the human race?"

"Do you really think that with all of the pollution we pump into the atmosphere and the theft of the planet's natural resources, it wouldn't fight back to rid itself of the *disease* that's killing it? Like a surgeon cutting out the cancer?"

John attempted to speak, but Earl raised his hand and continued.

"With all of the new diseases, earthquakes, forest fires, and tornados popping up, you have to see that the world is fighting back. It's karma. Too many people are on the planet with no respect for what it can do for us. What it *is* doing for us. Nature's a bitch, 300 million killed off in the 20th Century from smallpox alone, the Spanish Flu wiped out nearly 100 million during the Great War, the Black Death, 75 million over 300 years." He paused again, hand still up. His index and forefinger started to wiggle. "Jake set me up with a butt."

Jake threw a cigarette at him without missing a beat. Earl lit it and continued. "And we're not much better; nearly 60 million people killed during the Second World War. Brutal statistics - but necessary? You bet! With fewer people to shelter and feed, the planet isn't hit as hard by mankind's abuses. There are too many people on Earth right now, so you can expect to see one of two things happening soon: war or global retaliation. Read Malthus, man; it's all there in black and white. My money's on war. Look at the history of the world – did you know that in all of recorded history, there have been only seven days of peace? And that's seven in total, *combined*, taking an hour here, a few minutes there. War has been controlling the population ever since we learned to fight.

"So, in answer to your question, Caroline: yes, we need world wars. Imagine the damage the planet would unleash if we didn't have them. The unfortunate thing about a worldwide war is that most life on earth would be devastated. That's why we never see countries with nuclear weapons use them in battle. They're too efficient, too final. And the political implications of using a nuke could just as easily propel the planet into a world war. Every shithole country on the globe has a half-ass copy of the bomb now and won't be left out if someone decides to light one up."

"It looks like we have a member of 'The Four Horsemen' among us," Julia commented. The whole group laughed.

Caroline staged a rebuttal. "So, Earl, with the shape the world is in right now, you're suggesting that another war is imminent. Beyond population densities, on what do you base that profound prophecy?"

"Think about it, Caroline, everyone..." He paused for effect. "You've all heard of Revelations, in the Bible and the 'seer' Nostradamus. Not to mention the others who've seen the future, the *dark* future. They've all seen a third world war. Some say the 'war on terror' is the third and final installment of world wars. A third global war with nukes would end the world as we know it. Radiation would permeate the soil and the air. The lucky ones would be those who happened to be at ground zero when their city was hit. With history, fact, and the Bible backing up these arguments, I think I've pretty much covered my ass."

"I think you mean history, fact, and fiction, Earl. The *Bible*?" Connor shook his head. "Alright, I'm leaving this conversation." He struggled to stand.

"Connor," Sara broke in, annoyed, "The Bible is the most real thing in this conversation. I believe in the Revelations. I don't want to think it'll happen in my lifetime, but I believe it will one day."

"It's not a cop-out, Connor," added Earl. "It's as valid as anything you'll hear on the news today."

"It's ancient history, I mean *fictional* history. It's a piece of fiction. What can you draw on from the Bible that can make sense of the state of the world today?"

"It's not a complete work of fiction, Connor. It's steeped in historical fact, and you have to look into the past to see into the future. It's that simple."

"I think we're all too high right now to continue this line of thought," I announced.

"Joel!" Sara hissed. "I'm *serious*. Read it sometime. I guarantee you'll shit your pants."

"I was just saying that we should mellow out a minute. Don't get all worked up over nothing. You're not exactly a Bible thumper."

"I don't have to be a Bible thumper to believe in something, Joel!"

"Chill out," I went to grab her hand, but she pulled away. "Settle down."

I stared at Connor, amazed at Sara's attitude. He nodded and waved me over. On our way to the cooler, he settled me down with a show of acid.

"Just let her cool off, old man. You must have struck a chord or some shit." We snagged a beer each and sat on a large, protruding rock. "Do you want to do a hit?"

"I didn't know you brought more up." I licked my finger and dabbed it on the paper holding the acid. Connor followed suit with an impish smile.

While we waited for the drug to take hold, we listened to Kevin arguing with Sara over her *blind faith*.

"Faith is the key word there, Kevin." Her voice became louder. "That's why religions are also called *faiths*. Faith requires no particular proof." I followed her shadow with my eyes as the fire projected it ever closer to our position. "Faith is everything. I believe in heaven and hell with little more proof than the Bible can give me. I believe because I *want to*."

Kevin went silent. Sara was blowing this way out of proportion.

Sidney broke in. "Maybe you should read the Bible like Sara said. I skimmed through it once or twice in a hotel room while traveling, and the end of the book is, in essence, the end of the world." With this said, the whole group exploded in conversation.

"Intense, man," Connor sighed as he studied the stars. "And we wonder why wars break out over religion; these people are *friends*. Man, everyone has their own ideas on how someone else should live." A melancholy mood struck us both. I glanced over at him and saw him regarding me with vacant eyes.

Oh shit, *not again*.

For as long as I'd known him, Connor has had what some called 'second sight.' He could often sense that something was going to happen before it did. He told me once that his grandmother had had the same ability. Whenever one of those hunches struck him, his expression would go blank, and he'd stare off into space.

"Connor, if you're going into fortune-teller mode, keep it to yourself. I'm too buzzed, good or bad. Call me when it's over." I turned to leave, but my eyes hadn't adjusted to the dark, and I banged my head on a low-hanging branch. "Shit!"

He jerked as if electrocuted and watched me rubbing my forehead, his eyes slowly focusing. Then he started laughing, and so did I, relieved he was back without a grim premonition. We wandered into the trees, moving further from the noise, not stopping until the fire was a distant flicker. Finding a dry spot, we sat. Connor got cozy with the tree behind him, wrapping an arm around its trunk and resting his head against its rough bark. Moonlight lit our position through the treetops.

"This is a good tree. Put your hand on it, Joel."

I did, and the experience blew me away. A rush of energy shot through my body as my hand breached the tree's aura, an aura I swear I could see. Connor watched the expression on my face change as I connected with nature. "Good?"

"Insane." That was all I could say. Connor knew what I meant. I got up and began touching as many trees as I could. The phrase 'tree hugger' had just clicked. I giggled.

"Let's start a fire of our own," he suggested. "What do you think?"

"Good call, but I think everything is wet from the storm this afternoon."

"We'll find dry wood somewhere." He rose with a grunt. "These are birch trees. We'll peel their bark for kindling. It burns well. You got a knife?"

"No, but I have a lighter."

"No worries." As I resumed my love-in, I could hear the bark being torn from their trunks.

A skunk crossed my path a moment after I left Connor. It was not a bizarre thing in the north woods, but this was no ordinary skunk. My brain, still working on some intuitive level, recognized the threat before me. I froze. Raising my hands slowly, I massaged my eyes and prayed the image would disappear. "No, no, no...."

Unfortunately, the scene did not diminish. In fact, it got more freakish as my vision focused. The skunk had positioned itself on a dead stump and stared at me with an urgency that sent me reeling. My heart stopped as I gazed upon the animal's distinctive and familiar abnormality. One front leg was shorter than the other.

He stood on his hind legs like a puppet. Suddenly, light from an unknown source illuminated his stage. "Joel, you know who I am," he said. "You need to know why I am here. Please, don't be frightened; I am only a vision."

I cut him off.

"You're right about that!" I pointed an accusing finger. "You're nothing more than a vision. And a bad one at that."

I'd lost any ability to move and fell to my knees in trying. Now face to face with the talking skunk, sure I had lost my grip on reality, I could only listen. It was all so very real, palpable. I giggled at the thought, shaking my head. "Joel, please, you must know. You must be prepared...."

Before he could say more, Connor's voice broke the spell, and the skunk ran off.

"Joel! So th! is where you went." He slapped me on the back and knelt beside me. "Freaking out a little? Don't love it too much, man."

The feeling had returned to my legs, so I stood. "You have no idea, buddy. No idea. I just had a conversation with a skunk. Explain that to me."

"Cool. Acid agrees with you. You followed your hands around the night of the beer gardens as though they were blazing a path for you." He led me back to our new fire. "What do you think? There wasn't a lot of dry wood, but it's cooking now."

I sat. Then, pondering the events that turned an otherwise good trip into a nightmare, I clutched my stomach and threw up all over my shoes.

Chapter Seven

"Whoa, you sick, Joel?" Connor, now laughing, picked me up and assisted me to the water's edge. Taking off my shoes, I threw up again. "Let's get you back to camp."

"Sorry, man," I groaned. "That vision messed me up." I remained by the lake while Connor went back to extinguish the fire. Feeling confident I'd finished puking, I dragged myself to dry land and disrobed.

Back at the camp, the group was going strong except for Jake, lying in someone's lawn chair, a bag of pot on his lap. Sonny, John, and Caroline had pushed their chairs together and were howling over some joke. Freddy crawled into his tent with a beer and a magazine. Sidney and Julia read a newspaper by flashlight while Tom stood close enough to be part of their conversation but not have to contribute to it. Kevin lingered at the water's edge, chatting with Gil and Seth while Earl concentrated on keeping the fire hot.

"Look whose back!" Earl announced. "Thought we'd lost the two of you."

Everyone turned. Sara's head poked out of our tent. I waved, wiping my mouth. Then I looked down at myself, remembering I only had my boxers on.

Noting everyone's stares, Connor spoke in my defense. "What? He went for a swim." He leaned toward me and whispered, "Why don't you throw on something dry. I'll set us up with a nightcap." I shook my head. I wasn't ready for bed.

After assuring Sara that all was well, I joined the diehards at the fire. The group, now quiet, gazed at the night sky. I followed suit and picked my star. I'd noticed something strange, though: the earth seemed still. The mood was right, and the sky was clear, so I should have been cruising through the universe on my little planet, secure in the passenger seat. What was wrong? I felt panic set in. Next, black soot began to fill my field of vision, floating silently down all around me like dirty snow. I swatted at the flakes as they fell on my shoulders and in my hair.

Was it from the fire? No, no one else was being bothered by it, though it fell on them as well, their shoulders, their laps, and their feet. I closed my eyes hard. Opening them again, I found that all had returned to normal.

"I could see it too." Jake confided in me.

Shivers ripped through my body. I sat up slowly. "See what?"

"The... snow?" He paused. "The black snow." He pointed a hesitant finger above my head.

"You *saw* it?" I was floored.

Jake rubbed his eyes hard. Then he massaged his face roughly. He was now waking from his drug-induced nap. He steadied himself and lit a cigarette. Seeing that the drink at his side was still full, he took a nervous swallow. Scanning the ground and the group, he realized what he'd experienced hadn't happened. "Just what - what did I *see*?"

I retreated tactfully. "Jake, I was just messing with you, buddy. I don't know what you're talking about." A forced smile followed the lie. Jake squirmed a bit in his seat. Then he began to laugh.

"I must be over the edge tonight, man." Jake continued to laugh, chalking the vision up to substance abuse. "I'm FUCKED!"

Sonny scowled. "Yeah, we know you're *fucked*, you idiot. Now shut up before I knock you out. You're ruining my trip."

Connor was now staring at me from across the fire with that damn look on his face, that *knowing* look. "Something going on? You want to tell me anything?"

Get outta my head, Connor. That's what I wanted to say to him. Actually, I would have loved to tell them all about what I'd just witnessed, but doing so would have gotten me tagged as a whack job or an asshole. No thanks. For all I knew, I was having a bad acid trip.

"Jake was just freaking out over something he thought he saw. I'm fine."
I could tell he wasn't buying it, but he let it go.

Connor's pipe came out next, James Bong, and made its rounds.
Remembering my last vision, I quickly focused on the soil surrounding my
bare feet. Playing with it soothed my anxiety.

Gil, Seth, and Kevin returned from their nighttime stroll in the forest.
"We spotted a nasty cloud south of our position, blacker than the sky,"
Seth reported. "We should bear down for a crazy storm in about an hour
or so."

Gil nodded as he gestured at a fine mist drifting off the water into our
midst. "The wind's picking up off the lake, blowing this fog to shore. The
cloud`s also blotted out the moon."

"You should be pleased, Joel," Added Kev, remembering my love of
storms. "This one should be a competitor."

Connor challenged me. "Going to ride this one out? Sounds like a rough
one." He was pushing my buttons. If I could stay up for another hour, I
would fight it. I shook a lame fist at the sky. Nature's power. I respect it;
that's why I challenge it.

*****

Gazing up at the ominous sky, I remembered a time, not long ago, in the
forest behind my house, facing a storm of similar size and fury. Connor,
Earl, and Jake were with me - before Jake had ruined his life. The wind
was wreaking havoc on the treetops and screaming through the fields,
ushering in the rains. We stood our ground, leaning into the powerful
gusts, shielding our faces with our hands and shirts.

We'd been playing war games all afternoon. No one had successfully
ambushed anyone else the whole day, so I tuned into channel three on
our walkie-talkies and directed everyone to emerge from their positions
and rethink our game strategy. They came, trigger fingers ready, when
BOOM! Thunder crashed in the distance. We cringed. A wind pounded
through the trees, knocking Jake on his ass. This gale had twister
characteristics, so we planted ourselves.

"So, what do we do? Stick it out?" Connor shouted against the howling
winds. The rain was getting thick, making it hard to see the person in
front of you. It was even harder to hear anything. About ten seconds later,
the wind changed direction drastically, now pulling rather than pushing.
Then it all came to a screeching halt: the wind, rain, all of it.

Drenched to the bone, we looked at the devastation around us, wondering
how we'd survived it unscathed. The forest was a mess. All around us,

trees were split or uprooted – only the largest or the youngest remained. Yet not one of us incurred a single injury. Later, we learned that we'd survived a mini twister that had killed five cows and injured twenty others in the area.

It made you wonder. Ever since that fateful day, I'd challenged every storm that came my way. Connor was the same. Earl considered himself lucky but didn't invest any deeper meaning into it. Jake, I think, just had the shit scared out of him.

*****

Half an hour had passed without a word from the circle. We listened to the wind sweep the fog past our camp. Thunder soon broke our trance, obscure and still very distant. I glanced in the direction of my tent as Sara wandered out. Looking around and rubbing her eyes, she noticed me rooted to my chair. I smiled. She came over and planted herself on my lap, wrapping her warm arms around my neck. I kissed her exposed shoulder while she pulled her fingers through my matted blonde hair. We were back.

The rain never arrived. It could be heard on the far side of the lake, keeping its distance. We joked about how the storm didn't want to challenge us to a fight tonight. Waiting made everyone tired. Some slept in their chairs while others made it to the safety of their tents. Ending the weekend was tough; no one wanted to be the first to crash on the last night. It was hard to let go of a good thing.

Chapter Eight

We awoke to a sticky, humid morning. Fog still hung at knee level, but at least we could see in front of us. A heavy grey cloud had replaced yesterday's stunning blue sky. Wiping my face desperately to keep the sweat out of my eyes, I acknowledged the humidity was fierce.

Sara and I had completed loading the truck and now waited for the others. Kevin was attempting to wake up Jake, who, we suspected, could end up dead one morning, to no one's surprise. Gil and Seth had been up for a few hours- they were at the lake catching and releasing their last few fish while Tom and Sonny made coffee for the crew. Freddy was out purging himself, as unbelievable as that might seem on a day like this, while Sidney, John, and Caroline loaded up John's car. Earl was busying himself with his truck, fixing a leak: always something wrong with that truck. Connor and Julia returned from a nature walk, reporting a Freddy sighting.

"As he darted by us, he said he'd be back in a half hour. One more lap around the forest, I guess." Connor shook his head, giggling at Fred's determination to be the picture of health.

"He can't be serious. It's so humid."

Gil came back from the lake, fishing rod in hand. "No fish today." He looked puzzled. "I can't understand it. We did so well this weekend."

I bit my lip as my heart skipped a beat. Gil added, "And that damn cloud's still hanging in the south." He pointed in its direction.

A pain in my chest ignited an anxiety attack. I squeezed Sara's hand a little too tightly. She pulled free, rubbing the reddened skin. "Joel, what's the matter?"

"Sorry... I didn't mean to..."

"You need some downtime. This weekend took a lot out of you." She smiled. "When we get home, I'll make you some soup, run you a bath, and tuck you in, alright, lover?"

"Okay." I relaxed. We kissed. A hug followed, long and deep, melting into each other. She was such a comfort.

The group was ready to go by 12:30, so we reluctantly began the long ride back to civilization. The fog cleared as we drove further from the lake. Pulling out of the forest and back onto the main road, which would take us home, we spotted the dark cloud hanging ominously overhead.

Silence governed conversation during the drive. Connor's radio picked up only static, and we were all too tired to say much. An hour into the three-hour trip, we pulled into a gas station. As we gassed up, anyone with a full bladder took advantage of the facilities. I wandered into the store to talk to the attendant and hopefully get an update on the Reaper's activity.

"Nope, can't say," replied the old man behind the counter. "Our TV and radio have been all screwy since I got up this morning. Must have something to do with that storm cloud there." He pointed out the window. "Not a lot of traffic either, not since yesterday. Come to think of it, yesterday I saw more people pass through here, headed north, than I've seen on most long weekends."

"Alright, thanks." I pushed through the heavy glass door, disheartened at the lack of information, and approached Connor, who was still pumping gas. "This guy's radio is out too. He's blaming it on the cloud." I paused. "I'd say he's right."

"No worries, buddy." Connor was in good spirits. "Get in the truck. I'll pay the man, and we'll go."

When we were on the road again, I fought the urge to tell Connor to turn around, to take us anywhere but home. I couldn't explain it. I told myself that the hovering cloud was the product of an early summer storm and that what the skunk had told me was nothing more than acid-induced bullshit. I fidgeted in my seat, feeling hot and anxious. Connor agreed that it was unusually warm and turned on the air conditioning.

Another hour and a half and the cloud was on top of us – that's when vast flakes of what looked like snow began to fall. Connor's wipers fought valiantly to clean up our field of vision as the flakes became thicker. The washer fluid steamed as it hit the windshield, lubricating the wipers and muddying our view. Connor finally pulled off the road, got out, and tried to clean the window himself with a rag. After a couple of futile wipes, he hopped back into the truck.

"What is this shit?" He brushed it out of his hair and off his collar. "Look at how my wipers are dragging along the windshield. Everything's so *hot*, and the visibility is really starting to suck." The wiper squeaking against the streaking windshield was becoming irritating.

"It looks like ash." Julia offered. "Not to alarm anyone, but I was in Costa Rica when the Arenal Volcano erupted, and this is exactly what it looked like a few minutes later. Maybe there's a forest fire somewhere, burning out of control." She reached out the window, collected a specimen in her hand, and studied it. "This is some pretty big ash, though."

Sara's voice trembled. "Just don't go back out in it unless you have a rag or something to put over your mouth and nose. We don't know what this stuff is. It could be from a chemical plant that burned down somewhere."

We stared at each other, anxiety and confusion visible on our faces as we tried to figure out what was happening. The silence was broken when John knocked on Connor's window.

"I'm not going to ask you guys what the hell's happening here, but I suggest we get to cover as soon as possible." He glanced back at his vehicle, covering his face and head with his hands.

"Okay, let's go to Joel's house and wait this out. We can call our houses from there. That cool, Joel?" Connor looked at me, his jaw muscles flexing.

"Sure, my place is closest. Let's do it."

John nodded. "I'll tell the rest of them."

Sara handed him a T-shirt from her bag. "Put this over your mouth, John: to be safe."

He thanked her, then ran back to his car, his jacket pulled over his head and his T-shirt pushed into his face.

Trying my best not to panic, now sure of what had happened, knowing the source behind the dirty snow, I turned and smiled at the girls. "It'll be alright... We're almost home."

Connor stepped on the gas, and we rocketed back into action. During the final approach home, we ran into a brand of traffic only a farming town could throw at you. A herd of panicked cattle was pouring onto the road, pushing into one another as they squeezed through the narrow opening in the downed wooden fence. Once again, our motorcade was forced onto the shoulder. Thank God the stampede ended quickly enough, and soon we were moving again. I thought of my neighbor - did he know that his livestock had broken free? The trees were on fire behind his house; perhaps that was what spooked the cattle. What if the forest behind my house was going up in flames? Or my house!

"I gotta clean the window again." Connor pulled over and got out while we remained in the car, craning our necks to see out the windows. A deafening sound came from above. I spotted a low-flying plane, a fat-bodied military one. A Hercules? Water poured from its belly, smothering the flames behind my neighbor's house. That was a reassuring sight. Then we saw six more flying just over the tree line, heading north. They released a massive payload on the forest just behind my house and continued on.

"See that!?" Shouted Connor, throwing himself back into the driver's seat. "Must be some serious forest fire causing this cloud!"

"Maybe that's all it is." I heard myself say. "Let's get to my house and turn on the generator. I want to see if we can get a channel on the satellite. There has to be a station covering this." Our caravan sprang back into action, plowing through the ash collecting on the roads.

The yard looked slightly scorched but otherwise normal. But my house! My house was burning! Wait, no, it's just steam billowing off the clay shingles. I made a mad dash for the front door. Everything was as I'd left it, except for the acrid smell of chemical smoke that permeated the rooms. The others still assumed that the culprit was a large forest fire. Not me. I knew differently. I *knew*, but I didn't want to believe it.

As we piled into the house, Connor rushed to the basement and immediately turned on the generator.

All my friends lined up for the phone, as none of their cell phones had reception. Nobody got through the first time around. Fear crept into our circle – I could see it in their eyes. I left the group at the phone and hurried to my room, where I looked out the window.

Seeing the devastation in the back woods sent my heart racing. Several large trees were stripped of their branches, naked to the soot and falling ash. I figured that the water from the planes tore the smaller branches from their trunks. While I watched, an inky darkness crawled over the sky, turning afternoon into night.

Someone was calling for me from the main floor. Turning away from the alien view, I went downstairs.

"The phone doesn't seem to be working, Joel," said Caroline. "We'll have to go home to see what's up."

"Alright." Raising my voice, I addressed the troops. "If you guys want to head home and ensure everybody's okay, go. I'll wait here but come back tonight and let me know… so I know."

Freddy spoke up. "I don't think it's smart to go back out in this. Not until the smoke clears."

"Well, I'm worried about my family. I need to know they're alright." Caroline insisted.

"It's only a twenty-minute drive to any of our houses from here," John added. "I think we'll be able to get safely there and back. Then we'll know." His voice trailed off, his anxiety audible.

"Maybe, but if you want, you can stay here. I'm going to try the TV." I passed through the crowd into the living room, wiped the endless beads of sweat from my face, and turned the television on. Nothing. Not even the local station was on the air. The satellite was affected by the heavy ash in the atmosphere. Switching to antenna didn't help. "Damn!" I turned to Connor. "Try the stereo."

He fiddled with the switch. "Nope. Something's up. We'd all better go to our parents' places and see what we can see." He pushed past Gil and Seth, and they followed. I was close behind.

"If something bad has happened, promise me you'll all come back." I pleaded. I hugged Sara tightly before sending her off with Connor and Julia. Shaking Connor's hand, I added, "Come back before too long, either way, you know?" He nodded, and the whole crew exited.

I tried the television again, leaving it on a single channel, just in case. If nothing more, the white noise would suffice as company. Then I remembered the internet: odds were it would still function! But as I sprinted for my room, I realized that there would be no Internet access if the satellite were down. "Damn it!" My stomach tightened into a fist.

Another possible resource came to mind. The paper- perhaps there had been some warning. After all, the old man at the gas station had mentioned seeing heavy northbound traffic yesterday. We had the local paper delivered daily, so the Saturday edition should still be in the mailbox at the end of the driveway. I wore a heavy jacket and raced outside, pressing a dish towel against my nose and mouth. Sure enough, the paper was stuffed tightly into our box. I pulled it out and ran back to the house.

After throwing the ash-flecked jacket off, I went to the kitchen, slammed the paper down on the table, and sifted through the bloated inserts from the new superstore. Then, my worst fears were realized. I had that moment of terrible clarity when my future and the futures of those remaining were laid out before me.

The headline read "The Reaper Cometh". I now knew that this was it and that my friends would return with dire news of their own. I read on. The Reaper had confirmed that he had more nuclear missiles in his personal arsenal than first feared. The story also explained what one should do if the Reaper followed through on his threats: where to go, how to stay safe, and how to fight against the radiation poisoning that would be sure to follow.

I knew it had happened, but I still had hope. After all, *we* were all still alive. The worst-case scenario flashed through my head, and I did what little I could to control it. Wait and see.

Waiting for the door to open was unbearable, so I kept busy with mindless chores. Again, my attention returned to the paper. A new statement had been posted on The Four Horsemen website - this one directly from the head Horse's mouth. The paper had published it. "Blame your governments, blame your greed, blame your ignorance and your ambition. Blame yourselves for your end." It was chilling.

A bout of nausea struck me, sending me to the bathroom. I just knelt there, hugging the toilet and staring into the bowl. Like Nostradamus looking into his water bowl to see the future, I sat looking at mine. Finally, I stood and slowly made my way back to my room.

The clock on the wall read four in the afternoon. Funny, it felt like midnight in the seventh circle of hell. How long would it remain midnight here? I passed my parents' room en route. I still called it *their* room, as though Dad was still alive.

Stepping into my room, once a sanctuary, I went to the window again and pressed my hands against the glass. It was warm. I pulled away and rubbed my palms together, never breaking my gaze. A feeling of hate overcame me. The Reaper was responsible for *this*; that piece of shit had thrown the world into the gutter! Who the hell did he think he was? I could feel my face tighten. "Fuck!" My fist hit the wall beside the window. "Fucker!" I sank to my knees, continuing to punch the wall on my way down. When I reached the floor, it became my target until the mood left me on my knees, slumped over, crying for all things lost.

After several minutes, I pulled myself together and got up, but I stumbled, knocking over Rex. When I picked him up, his tail fell off. I tried repositioning him, but he would no longer stand without the tail. Sighing, I sat Rex next to me on the bed.

Then, I surveyed the rest of the house for damage. My rounds began with the bathroom, where I ensured the toilet flushed and we had running water. The next stop was the addition, where I observed that Kevin's paintings remained intact. My gaze fell on his latest piece, the one from my recurring dream. It sat unfinished on his easel.

I tried again in the living room to access a radio broadcast. No luck- maybe the reception was still messed up. Or maybe I was just full of wishful thinking. But there had to be other survivors in the area, right? We saw the planes in the sky- a sign that others made it too. I turned away from the radio and mused, "Actually, they may have seen us driving here as they put the fires out, and they'll come looking for us!"

I settled on the sofa, cherishing the image of a brilliant rescue until I was relaxed enough to sink into a restless slumber.

Chapter Nine

I dreamed, although all I could remember afterward was disjointed imagery. I saw body parts: first a leg, then an arm. A torso and a hand. The wing of a bird. A horn like that of a mountain goat. When I tried to make sense of it, I concluded that my subconscious was reconciling the lost link between man and nature.

My throat tickled as I sat up. When I coughed, something dark and thick spattered onto my hand. I'd inhaled some of the crap that fell from the sky. Maybe it was to blame for the messed-up dream, too. The front door opened as I ran into the bathroom to spit the rest of it up.

"Joel!" Connor shouted. "You alright?" His voice cracked as if he'd been crying. "Sara's here too, and so is Julia."

I wiped my mouth and hurried to meet them. Connor was setting his bags on the entry hall floor while the girls hovered in the open doorway, clinging to each other. "Looks like we'll be staying here." He said. His head dropped, and my heart sank.

I squeezed his shoulders, and he didn't need to say anymore; I knew. Then I approached Sara. I wanted to rescue her, to erase the terrified expression from her eyes. She released Julia and clung to me.

"Oh, Joel," she half-sobbed. "It's awful, it's so awful...." She began to weep. I held her a little tighter. Julia hugged Connor from behind, her cheek resting against his back, but he seemed stiff, unresponsive. Maybe he was in shock.

"I've got to get the rest of our stuff out of the truck." He muttered before venturing back outside.

"They're all dead, Joel," whispered Sara. "My family, the whole town..." She broke down again.

It was hard to keep my tears in check, but I managed. "I'm sorry, Sara, I'm so sorry.... but we'll be alright. We'll be alright." That seemed like such a weak thing to say, but it was all I could think of. "Look, would you mind giving Julia a hand? I have to take care of something."

She understood - I needed to go to Connor and snap him out of whatever had him acting like a robot. Releasing her gently, I took a heavy parka from the front hall closet and threw it on to protect myself from the ash.

I found Connor in the truck, just sitting in the driver's seat, staring blankly ahead. Climbing into the passenger side, I asked gently, "Connor, you okay, buddy?"

He didn't move his head. "It's brutal, Joel. The roads are congested, full of cars that don't go anymore. People are dead in the streets. I couldn't find anyone at my house; maybe they got away." He finally looked over at me.

"Maybe," I said. Then I turned away, studying the windshield. "The Reaper did it, man. He did exactly what he said he'd do. The local paper picked up the last thing he'd written on the net. This isn't the end, though, Connor. The military planes, the ones that put out the fires, they *saw* us. They'll probably be back to pick us up. They might have even picked up your parents and brother."

My words seemed to have an effect. Some life warmed his eyes, and his rigid expression relaxed. "Yeah, maybe. Yeah...."

"Let's get this stuff into the house," I suggested, gesturing to the back of the truck. Anything to keep him from slipping back into a funk. We loaded up and hurried back inside through the curtains of ash.

"The others should be here soon," I told everyone after closing the door and dropping my load on the floor. "Let's keep busy. Sara, take your stuff into my room. Connor, take yours, and Julia's into the spare. We've got to make room for everyone." While they complied, I remained on the main floor, lighting candles, mind racing.

Our tasks completed, the four of us sat coupled up on the pull-out chairs in the living room. None of us wanted to be alone. Connor and the girls recounted the horrors they'd seen on the streets and in their homes. Outside was a war zone. Death surrounded us now.

"We went to each of our houses together, so none of us had to be alone." Connor wiped his eyes. "I covered up the ones we found, the dead. Then, I took the stuff I thought we needed. Only what we needed."

Julia whimpered into Connor's shoulder. He put his hand on her head.

"There's more useful stuff out there, in other people's houses and stores. We should check it out before... Well, we should check them out soon."

I nodded, knowing that he meant before those left to loot cleared everything of value out. "The others will bring supplies too. Then we'll take stock and see what else we need."

No more was said until the door again flew open. Earl could be heard bitching as he pushed his way into the house.

"Joel, Connor, you guys in here?" He spoke clearly: nothing in his voice hinted that he'd endured the horrors the others had. We rounded the corner anxiously to greet him, sliding on the tile in our socks.

"Earl!" I took a box from him while Connor helped with the bags. "Nobody left at your house either; I take it?" What else could I say?

Earl sat down at the kitchen table. "Oh, there were people, alright: *dead people*. But people all the same."

Connor held his shoulder and led him into the living room. "Sorry, there's no good way to state the obvious. You want to talk about it?"

"No. But we need to start thinking about tomorrow." I thought I heard a light giggle escape him. "I got more shit out here if you want to help."

"Sure, be right with you," I replied. When Earl left the room as quickly as he'd entered it and ventured outside, I beckoned to Connor. "What was *that*? Should we be seriously concerned about him? That was creepy."

"Hey, what do we know, right?" Connor raised his palms. "Everybody's going to react differently to this."

Sara spoke up. "That response was *not* normal, Joel. I don't think he's all there."

"I know, but he's dealing with his family's death. He'll snap out of it."

"We have to get him to talk. To grieve is the only way to get past it. It's unnatural to block it out. It'll blow up in his face."

"Sara, let it go." I squeezed her shoulder gently. "It's his call, not ours, to make for him." After kissing her forehead, I joined Connor and helped Earl with his baggage, including a mini arsenal.

"*Jesus*, Earl, getting ready for that third world war?"

He stopped and gently pulled me aside. "Joel, look around you; the war's over." He pointed toward town. "This cache is for the aftermath. For the survival of our group. I won't end up like the others; I am *not* ending up like that. Poor fuckers. I raided the gun shop on Elm: figured the stiffs in there couldn't use 'em no more, so I grabbed everything I could carry."

"Well, let's hope we never have to use them. A good precaution, though."

"Oh, I was going to get more. There was a lot more than this: guns of all models, bows, crossbows, animal traps. Shit, Joel, I'll have the perimeter of your property so well guarded a squirrel won't make it in."

"You hearing this, Connor? Earl's calling martial law." I picked up a gun and pointed it skyward. "Shit."

Suddenly, we heard a car skidding to a halt on the wet gravel outside, followed by a snapping sound. We rushed to the garage entrance, but visibility was poor.

"Can you tell who it is?" I asked.

"We'll have to go out there to see," Connor replied. "That didn't sound too good."

We adjusted our parkas and ventured into the smoke. Just then, three figures approached from the darkness, bags in hand.

"God damn it!" It was Freddy's voice. "Earl, is that you?"

"Damn straight. Who else have you got?"

"It's me, John, and Caroline's with me too." They were close enough now for us to see them clearly.

"Hi, guys." Caroline was a mess. Ashes streaked her hair and face, and she clutched a backpack for dear life. "Are Sara and Julia here?"

"Yeah, they're in the house. Come on in."

"What the hell happened to your brakes, John?" Earl asked as we filed inside. "Sounds like you almost missed the place."

"John drove like a champ," Freddy defended. "We almost went off the road ten times. His brakes aren't shot; it's the roads. That ash - it's brutal."

Kevin and Jake were the next to appear. Bags in hand, their faces indelibly marked by what they'd seen. Soon afterward, Gil and Seth showed up.

They were crushed, we all were, but Gil seemed to show it more sharply. There was a black melancholy about him that made you uneasy. He chain-smoked, hands quivering, while Seth spoke.

"There are definitely survivors out there, but that's not necessarily good news. We saw two guys beat another for his loot. I'm pretty sure it was Danny and Donny. You know, those two *dicks*. People like that are going to use this as an excuse. We saw others pouring out of the church on Wellesley, too. Not sure if it was a riot or what. Then, there were shots fired in the distance. I'm afraid the violence is escalating out there, and we'll have to be just as ruthless to stay alive."

Sara broke in. "You make it sound like we'll have to kill to survive." She was as white as a shroud.

"I just know that if we can't do the same - if only in self-defense — we're already dead." Seth scanned the group as though looking for a weakness in our lines. "They're killing each other in the streets! We have to defend ourselves."

"Agreed." Earl didn't need persuasion. "We must accept that people will not be the same after this. I brought the guns and ammunition here for that very reason."

I lifted my hand. "Let's just settle down a minute. What Seth and Gil witnessed tonight may only be people's initial reaction to the situation. However, it does make sense that people who are hungry and frightened will do anything to remedy that. We can't take on any more people here other than Sonny, Sidney, and Tom. We don't have the resources, so yes, we will have to defend our property from those who'd take it from us." I looked at Earl. "I want you to scope out the best positions in the house to monitor the property."

He jumped out of his seat and went to work. I then addressed everyone else. "I want you all to keep watch but also keep your heads. We're in a pretty obscure spot up here, and I doubt we'll ever meet up with anyone else, with the hopeful exception of the military. I believe they saw us pull in here today and will return to help us."

Connor spoke up. "We don't know what's in store for us, and the more prepared we are for the worst, the better off we are in the end. Gathering supplies and hoarding food and water should be the top priority tomorrow morning. Meats and dairy won't be edible in a few days if we don't get it back here and in the cold cellar. Smoke as much of the meat as we can."

"Good thinking," I agreed. "We should go back to town and see what the grocery stores can offer."

"How was it at your house, Seth?" John asked. "Was anybody left?"

"Not a soul. I'm hoping they got out with the others who went north."

Gil kicked the wall and lit up another cigarette. Seth placed a soothing hand on his arm. "I'm afraid Gil's experience didn't give his family as much hope." He explained. "My house was empty, but Gil's was full. It was like half the town had come to his place - to die."

Gil whimpered. Caroline hugged him.

"My parents were in bed when it happened." Kevin's voice broke. "I don't know, maybe they suffocated or something. Just died in their sleep. I wrapped them as best I could and made them comfortable. My sister was at her boyfriend's the night before last; I didn't see her. I left Dali with her before I came up to the lake, so I guess she's still with her..."

Then Julia volunteered the details of her nightmare. "My parents are divorced, so I only found my mom." She spoke slowly like she was still in shock. "I kissed her face. She was still warm, but maybe that's just because of the heat..." She trailed off. Connor's touch brought her back. "My dad lives hours from here. Maybe he's still alive. My baby brothers were with him this weekend. They have to be alive..."

"I think they all went quickly." Sara offered. "I know my family did. We covered them up when we arrived. Remember, Julia?" Her chin trembles. "Remember how peaceful they looked? It's as though they never saw it coming. Like Kevin's parents went in their sleep." She sank her face into my chest.

"When John, Caroline, and I first visited their houses, I prayed that somehow my house hadn't been affected like the others." Freddy clenched his fists. "Goddamn." His fist shot through the drywall. "Fuck!" He took a deep breath and then surveyed the damage. "Aw, Joel, I'm sorry, man."

Before I could respond with the story of the hole in my bedroom wall, we heard someone come crashing through the door downstairs. It was Sonny, and he was alone. No Tom, no Sidney. Earl had to pick him up off the floor. He was black with ash and shaking with anger.

"You alright, Sonny?" Earl asked.

"The hell kind of a question is that? I can barely breathe." He was the picture of an angry man who had revenge in his heart, not a man who had the images of dead family fresh in his mind. "Where's Joel? I need to tell him something."

"I'm right here, big guy." I helped him get his balance. Jesus, he was heavy.

"There's a group of people not far from your house. They're coming this way." A pause. "They've got guns."

Earl's expression turned grim. "So do we." He headed for the garage, followed by Connor and John. When they returned, Earl passed me a pistol.

I checked the clip. A reflex from Earl's firing range at the gun club. "Where are Sidney and Tom?"

Sonny stared. "They're not *here* yet? They left town way before I did. I stayed back to get my dad's van for the ride back. The two of them were supposed to come here together in Sid's car. That was a good two hours ago." Wiping the sweat and ash out of his eyes, he went on. "The damn van broke down on me about a kilometer from here, so I dragged most of my shit the rest of the way."

"Well, they haven't shown up, so something must have gone wrong." I glanced out the window, but all I could see was swirling ash and darkness. "How long before that group gets here, you think?"

"I figure about ten minutes. I passed them on the road up. Rowdy bunch- they shot at me."

"Let's hope Tom and Sid didn't run into those guys."

Sara approached me with a gun in hand. "Earl's showing everybody where to position themselves. He's asking for you."

I found Earl cracking open the south window in my parents' bedroom. He beckoned me over. "Stay right here, Joel. I will set the rest of our crew up around the house."

"Only fire if fired upon, okay, Earl? Promise me that. We don't know who they are. I know they shot at Sonny, but they're desperate and may have Sid and Tom."

Earl nodded and continued placing the troops. We were at war: the Reaper's actions were only the beginning. Now that we were facing our first possible battle, anxiety gripped me, testing me. I reminded myself that it wasn't just me; we were all fighting the same fear. "Breathe, just breathe, Joel," I told myself, focusing on the sweat dripping from my nose. I wiped it away.

"Joel, I'm with you." Jake tiptoed into the room. "Earl won't let me have a gun: he thinks I'm too screwed up. He doesn't trust me, so I'm gonna stay with you."

"Jake." I motioned for him to sit by the wall. "Where is he placing the girls? Where's Sara?"

"I think she's in the addition - he's got half the crew in there." Jake pulled out a smoke and lit it up. "Earl says that it's the best defensive spot in the house. He says we could hold off an army from up there."

He was taken with Earl's ability to command a situation like this. I was equally impressed. But I needed something to cool me down right now- I was still shaky. I approached Jake's cigarette and said, "Set me up with a drag, will ya?"

Jake handed it over. "You can have a whole one if you want. Me and Kev filled up on them before we came back. There must be a hundred cartons in his car."

"Don't get me hooked on one of your bad habits." I took a deep drag and handed the cigarette back. "Thanks."

"Fuck it, Joel, live it up, 'cause it don't look like we got much livin' left to do." A sad chuckle escaped him.

"Don't say that, Jake. We're going to be *saved*: the military will come for us. Until then, we'll defend ourselves and wait."

Jake just shook his head as if he didn't understand where this optimism of mine was coming from. Frankly, neither did I.

"Joel!" John shouted from the main floor. "Joel, get to the addition!"

I ran across the hall, Jake close behind me. "What, what is it?"

"They're here!"

Chapter Ten

Earl flew around the corner and headed up the stairs toward me.

"It's go time, buddy!" He declared. Grabbing me by the arm, he guided me into the addition.

"Can you see them?" He pointed to the end of the driveway while the others frantically blew out the candles. We peered into the dimness and saw some shadowy figures approaching the house. "They can't see us, not with our lights out."

Sonny's lips moved as he counted. "I think I saw six guys in their group when I passed them, but it looks like they've got eight or nine now."

They drew closer. I kept praying they'd turn back, but they continued. A familiar voice called out as I was on the verge of shouting a warning.

"Joel! Anyone there? It's me, Sid."

Behind me, everyone sighed with relief. Thrilled that another friend had returned safely, I opened the window further. "Is Tom with you?" I shouted back.

"Tom *was* with me, but we got separated. Listen, I'm coming in. I'll tell you everything in a minute."

Connor and I opened the front door with guns in hand. Sid staggered in while a dirty bunch of strangers remained on the porch, eyeing us warily.

"God, am I glad to see you guys!" He exclaimed. "Look, do you mind if we set these people up with some water? They've heard there's a migration headed north and only want to stop for a drink. They saved my life."

"Sure. Bring them in."

We set them up with a large cooler of water, which they gratefully accepted. Before leaving, they told us that a northbound pilgrimage was in progress, and they wanted to join it. I recalled that the military planes had flown north after they'd dumped their payload of water on the forest. They could be setting up a vast compound, collecting survivors. But how did these people know about it? What was driving them north? These questions hit me after their party departed, leaving me without answers.

"So, what happened? Where's Tommy?" Sonny asked sharply.

Sidney sat down at the dining room table. He looked exhausted. "After we left you, Sonny, we went to the grocery store to pick up what we could. Tom was having a tough time. You know Tom, he's a wreck. Nothing was easy to look at or accept, especially after we saw his house, right?"

Sonny nodded. "It was a total loss. We couldn't salvage anything."

"Yeah, well, I wish my house had burned to the ground too. Would have saved me from seeing what I saw." Sid swallowed hard and continued. "So, we were having a rough time with the bodies and all that on the street and in the store, but I was keeping it all down, right? Tom couldn't, he kept on puking 'til all he had left were the dry heaves. So, he's off puking for the tenth time as I was working the canned goods aisle, hoping to bring back some food for the house. Next thing I know, Tom's running out the far door, yelling for me to follow. Naturally, I high tailed it out of there. When he finally stopped, and I caught up, I asked why we were running. He tells me he'd seen the dead get up and lash out at him. *Like Zombies?* I asked him. He said they were grabbing for him. I just chalked it up to paranoia in the face of all that was happening; I think I might have even laughed. That's when he froze, and I took a look around me. We were being swarmed."

"So, what next? You both ran in opposite directions, and that's the last time you saw him?" Sonny asked, his voice tight.

"Hey, I reasoned with them the best I could." Sid looked offended. "When they got close enough, I recognized two of them. I'm sure one of them was my third-year soccer coach from when I was twelve. I pleaded with him to back off. Used his name and everything. Then I saw Mrs. Klein from the library. She was spouting some biblical bullshit. So, we're getting backed into a corner. I finally got through to Mr. Banks, the soccer coach. He explained they only wanted what I had, the box of food. I told him to go get blown. There was plenty to go around. He grabbed for it, and I hoofed him in the nuts. What I hadn't counted on was Tom *bailing* on me."

"You know he can't stand conflict; he probably just ran for cover."

Sid cut Sonny off. "Don't turn this on me, Sonny. I looked for him. I thought maybe he went back to your house, so I started for there. Then the pricks rushed me! I ran north, leaving the car behind, and dropped the food box. Shit, I felt bad about it, but Tom was gone, man." Sidney was losing his composure. "Then a shot rang past my ear, and they ordered me to stop. So I did." He rubbed furiously at his eyes. "Before they could do their worst, the group who brought me here scared them off. They told me where they were going and invited me to come along. I asked them to take me as far as here. Sonny, we fired at you thinking you were one of the assholes who attacked me and Tom. You almost ran us down."

Sonny shook his head. "Sorry, Sid, I couldn't see."

Sid plowed his fingers through his hair. Wet ash made for one hell of a mess, especially in Sid's short dreadlocks. "Listen, Sonny, Tom'll show up... He just got scared and ran." He pushed his chair back and stood. "All my stuff is still in my car in town. I want to get it back. Are there any plans to go soon?"

"We were planning on going there tomorrow morning," Connor replied, "but with all these assholes running around, I guess we'd better be armed."

I agreed. "We send five to town in the morning, and the rest stay here to protect the house. Sound good?"

"Perfect," Earl approved. "I volunteer for the trip. Who else wants to go to town?"

John, Sid, Sonny, and Seth volunteered to return to town, leaving the defense of the house to the rest of us. We did a time check after the meeting was over, and I suggested that we start taking showers one at a time, as many of us were covered in the filmy black soot.

"No longer than three minutes each. That way, water won't be wasted. We're on a well here, but remember, it's not bottomless." My mind raced with instructions on what to do in a crisis. "Keep the hot water to a minimum, too. We need to conserve what fuel we have for the generator."

"Meanwhile, let's get a schedule made up for 24-hour guard duty," Earl suggested. "It's important – for our defense."

And our survival.

*****

Freddy, Gil, and Sara took the inaugural guard shift while the rest of us went to our beds and couches and collapsed. The following morning, I was relieved for the 8:00 a.m. watch while Earl and the boys collected their gear for the drive to town. Julia insisted they tie wet rags to their faces to act as filters.

"Good luck, fellas," I said. "I'll see you in three hours." Then I added, "Come home with Tom."

Sonny shot a thumbs-up. "Count on it."

After they departed, the rest of us spent the morning taking stock of what we had to work with and noting what we needed. Fuel was critical to our survival, and conserving our present supply would be paramount. We would only turn the lights on when absolutely necessary. The fridges and freezer would run day and night as always. Anything else that used up batteries or made the generator consume more fuel would be carefully monitored.

What struck me as bizarre was the fantastic sleep I'd enjoyed the night before. The mental and physical stress combined had knocked me right out. Any dreams or nightmares that might have tormented me were not carried over into my waking memory. This made me almost feel like my old self again.

At 10:30 a.m., Connor approached me with the e.t.a. for our 'Away Team.'

"Half an hour, Joel, then I start to worry." He wiped the sweat off his bare chest with a towel. I was going shirtless, too. The girls had adopted a no-bra rule because the heat was just too much. There were no complaints from any of the guys.

I checked my watch. "Don't sweat it yet. Pun intended."

"Trying not to. What are you doing?"

"Trying to find some stuff we can use." I gestured at a dusty pile of boxes I'd pulled from the hall closets.

"Yeah, it's good to keep yourself busy." He stood over me, one leg shaking to an invisible beat. He was clearly nervous about something.

"You need to talk, Connor? You know I'm here for you. Just let me know."

"No, it ain't nothing. I'm going back up to see if Freddy needs anything."

"You're sure, man?"

He lifted his hands as if to say: It's all good. Then he left.

Upstairs, Freddy yelled that the boys were back. Connor hadn't made it halfway up the stairs before he was blazing a path back down. I opened the door. They were still exiting the vehicles, bags slung over their shoulders. I started a head count while Connor looked at me anxiously.

I shook my head. "Shit, I can't count them. It's too dark."

"Hey! Did you find him?!" Connor called out.

No answer, so we waited. The troops finally trudged toward the house, heads down and shoulders hunched against the pounding wind. When they came in, I managed a head count. Five, only five.

"Where's Tom?"

At first, they didn't answer. They glanced at each other and then at us, faces marked by discouragement and, yes, grief. "It's no good," Earl finally said. "We looked all over."

Sid lowered his head and grabbed his stomach. "Shit." Pushing his way past us, he ran to the bathroom.

Sonny clenched his fists. "I'm going back! I'm not finished!"

"Are you going back out right now, Sonny?" I asked.

"I wouldn't have even returned if I had taken my car." He never took his eyes off Earl. I half-expected him to start swinging, so I moved between them.

"Alright, I'll come with you." I guided Sonny to the front door and started preparing for the nasty weather. "Give us another three hours."

After I hugged Sara and promised to return on time, Sonny and I left the house. As we sprinted to Connor's four-runner, I felt the hot ash blowing on my neck. Breathing was difficult in this heat, even with the wet clothes on our faces.

The truck didn't start on the first try, but I'd driven this pig enough to know its quirks. The uneasy moment soon passed, and we were on our way.

Chapter Eleven

"Any new ideas on where we should look?" I asked, keeping my eyes on the road ahead.

"One." Sonny rubbed his hands together. "There's this place on the east side I remember him telling me about, behind one of those horse barns on the town line. He'd go there to think or some shit."

"So, we'll go there after we pass through town." I took a turn slowly. The ash build-up on the roads demanded caution.

Passing through town was a nightmare. The visual picture I had created from the others' descriptions did not do justice to the reality I now witnessed. Emotion almost got the better of me as we coasted past the twisted metal and fallen trees. Everything was scorched or burned to the ground. So many landmarks which had helped shape my young life were no more. I saw no movement through the shadows and smoke. Had everyone fled north? How would we ever find anybody in this? It seemed hopeless.

Sonny shook his head at me as our eyes met, scanning the debris. I accelerated and turned up Concession Ten at Sonny's urging.

We reached our destination after another twenty minutes on the road: a barn off the town line. It was then that the rain started to fall, black and heavy. Sprinting the final few meters through the devastated field, we despaired of finding Tom there until we noticed a mechanical hum from the barn.

Sonny pushed his way in first, helping me as I slipped in the mucky downpour. Once inside the barn's fragile shell, I removed my gloves and wiped my eyes clear. Sonny retracted his ski goggles and joined me at my side.

There was a veritable pot factory here, with hundreds of plants growing in their own bio-bubble. Tables lined the entire length of the barn in several rows.

"Eden!" Sonny had said a mouthful. I had to smile. The tell-tale leaves of the marijuana plants stood two to three feet above the wooden tables. These were full-grown specimens. The buds were huge, and their familiar scent permeated the barn's interior.

We walked softly on the concrete floor, careful not to disturb the perfect ambiance we'd stumbled into. It was an experienced set-up. Whoever had created this must have been growing for a government-ordered medicinal supply; that was my first impression. Upon closer inspection, I realized these plants were fed more than hydroponics. A well-known drug used to treat depression was also being pumped into them. This became apparent upon discovering dozens of labeled boxes and empty containers scattered on the floor next to the reservoirs.

Clay-growing chambers ran the length of each table, feeding the roots the cocktail of water, nutrients, and anti-depressants. The hum we'd been drawn to - we discovered - was a generator situated in the corner of the barn. It was connected to a large gasoline tank, similar to what we had at my house, vented through a small hole in the side of the barn. Six large reservoir containers stood before us. Five were full, according to their weight, as I set my shoulder against them and pushed. They were plastic cylinders painted black. I also noticed the temperature was very comfortable inside the barn. AC units hung from the rafters. Everything seemed to be on timers. The grow lights also hung low from the rafters on chains.

A nursery for the seeds to sprout in an inorganic soil compound was also set along the west side of the barn. A glassed-in cubicle about ten-by-ten feet housed a hundred seedlings in mini cubes. The grow lights were burning. The compound bags were scattered on the floor: Rapid Root brand. Several full bags were stacked against the wall.

It was very familiar as Sonny and I had researched a similar set-up online to replace the hillbilly operation we had outdoors.

"We should take all of this back," I exclaimed. "The plants look mature. No one else is going to smoke it."

Sonny just nodded. Then, remembering why we'd come, he shouted, "Tom! Where the Christ are you?" I nearly jumped out of my skin. His cry broke the tranquil aura we'd enjoyed upon entering the barn. At such a pained last attempt, I felt compelled to join in.

"Tom! Are you in here?!" No response. My heart sank.

After a few moments of eerie stillness, I set to work on our second objective by collecting the bud. After about seven or eight batches, I stopped and realized my jacket couldn't hold anymore. Sonny noticed and began to gather some of his own.

"Might as well get something outta this trip," he said, voice catching in his throat.

I found many clear plastic bags under a discarded trench coat and handed some to Sonny. We collected as many as we could carry and then drove the short distance back to the house.

Despite the mass disappointment over not finding Tom, everyone was curious about our discovery.

"How much weed have you got?" Connor asked.

"Fifty pounds." I speculated. "Maybe more. And there's more still in the barn. The best place for it is in the dry storage."

Connor discouraged this plan. He informed me the dry storage was now full of food from our first operation to town to locate Tom.

We decided on the garage instead. After clearing a dry shelf and stashing the bud, I pocketed enough to guarantee a few days of buzzed bliss.

"I'll smoke that with you." Connor noticed my sleight of hand.

"What do you say to a smoke show up in the addition? I think we could all use some time away from... well, we could use some time away."

He understood. "You want me to rally them? I'm sure they'll all be more than willing. We got booze, too; Earl hit the liquor store today."

"Okay then, let's do it!"

Half an hour later, we gathered in the addition, eager to force aside the bewilderment and fear that threatened to overwhelm us at any moment. Sitting in one of the few chairs available, I packed the pipe, a beer at my side- warm, but a beer all the same. I lit the pipe and inhaled heavily. The others were drinking and discussing the day's events. On the surface, the fact that we carried weapons now was the only distinguishing feature that this get-together was any different from the dozens we'd enjoyed in the past. The guns reminded me that this was just an attempt to punch holes in the darkness that enveloped us now.

I noticed Connor staring at me. I invite him over with a wave. He kneels beside me and nudges my arm with his elbow.

"You know you're our leader, right? They've decided."

"*Who's* decided? I'm nobody's leader."

"We had a sort of vote while you and Sonny were gone. I couldn't sway them to vote Jake in, but it was close." He smiled and took the pipe from me. "Why don't you say a few words? This is your party, Joel, your show."

"This is *our* show, Connor. I don't know if I like being voted anything."

"Just give them something to hang on to. Inspire them like you did the basketball team at the assembly last month. Remember?"

I take a moment to let the news sink in. I hadn't even considered making any one person the *leader* of our tribe. It meant a lot to me hearing it from Connor, though, the one person I would have voted for were I here. I stood up.

"Can I have everybody's attention?" I spoke slowly, distantly. This weed was very different from what I was used to.

My friends assembled around me. My head started to hum, and I felt the skin of my cheeks tighten as a considerable smile tattooed itself on my face. My eyes closed slowly. I began to scratch my face and hair lazily. The smile remained but transformed into a grotesque satire of itself. My scratching became more violently uninhibited, extending to my legs. I was completely unaware of what was happening around me now, interested only in the elusive itch. Not another word escaped my mouth for what I perceived to be five minutes. Then I sighed. "How long have I been scratching that itch?"

The laughter seemed to explode in my head. It was beautiful. I buzzed all over. James Bong did the job; now it was up to us to keep it unreal.

*****

The reasoning behind getting high tonight couldn't be disputed; it seemed almost ridiculous that we ever did before. Before this, I saw drugs as an escape, which begged the question: What was I trying to escape from?

A few hours into the evening, Gil became paranoid and had to have his gun taken away as a precaution. Nothing would bring the house down like an accidental shooting, so John suggested that we all relinquish possession of our firearms.

"Alright," I agreed, my high tapering off as the alcohol took effect. "John has a point! Guns are checked at the door when we come in here for recreation. This area is now deemed: Recreational." I finished by knocking my empty beer bottle on the window ledge- very Judge Joel of me.

"But Joel," Earl complained. "This is our best spot in the house for standing guard, what good is it..."

I cut him off.

"Earl, it's only when we're having fun; if someone is on duty here, they'll keep their gun. The others will leave theirs at the door." I scratched my face, feeling the itch return. Earl noticed and began to laugh and scratch at his chest. We all joined in. The laughter felt good and warmed us, unreal but real enough.

*****

The remainder of the night had its ups and downs. After all, this was only the second day of the new world, and my friends still had to get over their losses. Eventually, the addition, or 'Skylab' as we'd renamed it in our stupor, began to empty as people staggered off to bed. I thought our mystery pot had certainly come through in a pinch as I rolled the last joint of the night and sat against the east wall with Sara, Kevin, Jake, and Sonny: the diehards.

"Before we lose our buzz," I said, holding it up in front of everyone, "here's to... our futures..." I lit the joint and passed it around.

Sara was nodding off on my shoulder; I felt sleep encroaching also, so I relaxed and yielded.

Chapter Twelve

My head was heavy when I opened my eyes again, and I felt alone and disoriented. The room was dark. Realizing my hunger, I pulled myself up from the floor and exited Skylab.

A mental haze interfered with my locomotion and equilibrium as I moved through the house. I found it increasingly difficult to maneuver. A misplaced step in the dark, and I lost my footing, tumbled down the staircase, and landed in the front hall on my back.

Lying still as a corpse, I mentally scanned myself for shooting pains or some other sign of distress. Nothing. Slowly, carefully, I got up.

"Joel! Are you alright? Did you fall down the *stairs*?" Sara had heard the commotion, appearing at the top of the winding staircase. I gave her the thumbs-up.

"Just took the express route down." I caressed my ass.

"I'll do that for you." She grinned. "Come up to bed."

I double-timed it back up the stairs, forgetting food in a flash. Entering my room, I found the girl of my dreams lying in my bed, naked under the covers. She was as high as a kite. The pain had left her, if only for tonight. If only for tonight, we were who we were, the kids we were. That made me smile, to know the world outside was nonexistent to her right now, that it was just me and her in my room during any given evening in the first few days of an endless summer. I walked silently to bed, undressing along the way. Taking her face in my hands, I kissed her intensely. That night would not be the last of its kind by any means, but I can say that it was one of the most powerful memories I have of her, of us.

After an hour or more of almost animalistic passion, we lay there, slowly falling out of our fantasy and returning to the reality of where we were, of *when* we were. Sara spoke softly into my chest.

"I miss them, Joel... you know? I can't believe..." She couldn't continue. I hugged her tightly as she cried against me. "I miss them so much..."

"I know," I said. "I know."

She held me close and said what I'd known after our first encounter or had hoped I'd known. One thing was sure, though: it felt good to hear it.

"I love you, Joel. I really *love you.*" Our eyes met, and I broke down.

We embraced until sleep overcame us.

*****

I must have woken up five times that night. My blankets were all over the floor, except the comforter Sara had managed to hold onto. Shit, was it hot. My sheets were soaked, and I felt like a new river had opened on my forehead each time I woke. Trying not to rouse Sara, I sat up. Another nightmare troubled me, a new one. God, in how many different ways was my unconscious going to tell me I was 'not in Kansas anymore?'

This time, the images defied interpretation. I couldn't seem to pull a meaning from what I remembered. The problem was I couldn't remember enough to pull anything from it, save that it was bad.

My temples throbbed. I eased them with my fingers and then rubbed my eyes hard, producing flashes of white light. They, in turn, sparked a memory of the events leading up to my wakefulness. Despite the sweltering temperature in the room, I shivered.

Sara placed a hand on me. "Someone walk over your grave?" she asked, half asleep.

"What?" I asked.

"You shivered. It's an old saying: When you shiver, it means that somebody just walked over your grave."

"How could anyone have walked over my grave if I'm not dead?"

She had gone back to sleep, so my answer would have to wait until morning. My watch read 6:30 a.m. I glanced out the window, hoping to see the sunlight slowly brightening the sky. It was a knee-jerk reaction, I guess, one I wouldn't give up on too quickly.

*****

Earl knocked at our door minutes later. "Joel, you up yet? Your watch."

"Alright," I replied, coughing up a lung steak from the night before. "I forgot, be out in a sec." I maneuvered around Sara, careful not to wake her. Then I kissed her damp forehead and got dressed.

Earl was making his rounds when I reached the addition, checking all the windows and doors.

"Sleep in, Joel?" Caroline asked, gun at her feet as she sat in a patio chair facing the north windows.

"Guilty as charged," I replied. "I'm exhausted: I must have woken up a hundred times last night."

I grabbed a chair and sat at the east wall while Jake covered the west. I pulled the pistol from its holster, popped the clip out, double-checked that it was full, and forced the barrel back to ensure there wasn't a bullet in the chamber. "Anybody see anything this morning?"

"I ain't seen much," answered Jake. "So much rain, I can't see through it."

"I think the rain will keep people inside," added Caroline. "Earl went out for a minute to get something out of his truck and -" She stopped as Earl entered the room.

"The rubber on the wheels is starting to disintegrate – not good!" he reported. "It's brutal, man. At this rate, we won't have a vehicle that'll move from the driveway, and what's worse is we can't do anything to stop it."

I put the gun back into its holster and set it on my lap. "Can we fit them all in the garage?"

"Yeah, I was thinking that. I'll get the boys and start the move before more damage is done." He threw me a half-assed salute and walked off.

"Joel, hey Joel..." It was Jake, whispering under his breath. "You got some more of that pot?"

"I'm not giving you any, Jake."

There, I'd said it. He wasn't getting any weed unless a party was going on and most of us were partaking, never mind while on duty. His gun hand began to shake, and the sweat teetering on his eyebrows dripped, burning his eyes. I felt sorry for the poor bastard but was steadfast in not letting him slip away.

"Joel, I-I'm dying here, man. I really need something. I-I smoked and ate all my stash."

"Good. I don't want to worry about you being high and not doing your part."

It was tough love. I knew he understood the concept on some level, a level he'd forgotten. His gun hand shook a little more violently. I approached him.

"Jake, we couldn't do much for you in the past, but maybe now is the time." I knelt in front of him. His head dropped against his chest. "What do you say, Jake?" I took his rifle and put my hand on his upper arm.

"It's too hard," he whimpered, "I'm not worth it... It's too *hard.*" He raised his hands to his face and started to cry.

"You *are* worth it, Jake. Don't say that shit, man. You just lost control. You lost your way. I know we can get you back on track. I *know* it."

His eyes met mine, and compassion crippled me. I saw the Jake I grew up with, the friend who had shared his lunch when I had forgotten mine in sixth grade. This wasn't some burnout; this was Jake. This was my buddy Jake, who was a kind and giving soul before an awful accident took all that he was away from him. He'd never been able to talk to his father like I could with mine - leaving his mom. She was killed along with my dad in the untimely car crash that sent us both into therapy. The therapy did me a lot of good, but Jake couldn't get past the pain.

"No! God damn it! I don't *want to.* I don't *care* anymore... I don't *care.*" Now, he was pulling at his messy hair and sobbing. I held him awkwardly around the shoulders.

"Caroline, get Connor up here. I don't know what else to do." I begged. She wiped her eyes and hurried out of Skylab.

When Connor arrived, he sized up the situation immediately and produced a joint he'd not lit the night before. I nodded, and he handed it to me.

"Jake, I've got something that'll take the edge off. But know that this is not going to happen again." I gave it to him, hoping he'd decline the offer, but he snatched it eagerly. "Never again, if you smoke, it's because we're all smoking, never again on your own."

Through the frantic puffing, he thanked us. "My last one," he said, exhaling. "This'll take me..."

I stand and turn to Connor. "He wants to clean up."

"Clean up? No more drugs?" He almost laughed out loud. That angered me, and he felt it. "Sorry, but you're talking about..."

"Yeah, I know who I'm talking about. He's a mess and wants to change all of that."

While we discussed him, Jake consumed the whole joint in record time. He leaned back in his chair, and that blank, numb look crept over his face once more like a shadow.

"Hey, that's commendable, Joel. Don't get me wrong, I remember Jake, too, when he was more like us. He'd be a great addition to the group if he were clean. The thing is, this isn't going to be easy, what with the end of the world to work through and all."

I look down at him and shake my head. "I know, but he's reaching out. We should have done more for him before it got so bad. I should have done more..."

Connor interrupted me gently. "Don't go there again, Joel. We went through that two years ago."

"I'm not. I- I just think he wants help now."

Caroline spoke up. "Joel, I think Connor's right. Jake hasn't said once that he wants to quit. You *told* him he wants to, and it's my experience that you can't force someone to do something they aren't prepared to do."

My back went up when she said that, but reflecting on the conversation, I had to admit that my dialogue with Jake had been one-sided.

"Listen, I just think it's worth a chance. He's not this lost cause; there's more to this guy. You never really knew him when he was a regular guy, Caroline. He wasn't like this."

Jake remained in his chair, slumped over in stoned rapture. Hell, I'd have happily joined him, but then that was the difference between us: I knew when I could and shouldn't. Jake had lost that particular ability long ago.

"I'll stay and do his shift," offered Connor. "You have his gun?"

I handed Connor the rifle and reclaimed my seat.

An hour later, Kevin came through the door with a determined look. Everyone noticed. He marched to his paintings and grabbed a large pad of paper. Sitting on the floor, he began to draw painstakingly. I hadn't seen him inspired like this since before the weekend. It made me feel good like a piece of the past just barged in and reminded us who we were. I turned to Caroline to see her reaction. She was smiling and studying Connor's face; he was the only one close enough to see what Kevin was drawing. Suddenly, Connor's expression changed radically from an amused spectator to someone who'd just seen a ghost.

"Who is that supposed to be?" He asked. Kevin looked up at Connor and frowned thoughtfully before continuing to sketch.

"I'm not sure really," he answered. "I've been drawing him since I was a kid, but I haven't for a while now. I just woke up this morning and felt I had to draw him, to see him again." Kevin handed the pad to Connor. "My mom always said she thought maybe he was my guardian angel. She thought that was why his image would always come to me so clearly." Remembering his mother, Kevin flinched.

Connor studied the picture in his hands and then lifted his gaze to Kevin. "Then he's mine too."

"You know, some of the others have seen a similar drawing before." Kevin walked over to his pile of art in the far corner and sifted through several sheets and sketchbooks until he found an example. We were all standing in a semi-circle now surrounding the first drawing. He rejoined the group with three other portraits of the man he called his guardian angel. "I did these within the last four months."

We each took one and compared them to the most recent version. "Freddy saw this one last month and couldn't believe his eyes." He pointed to the one Caroline was holding. "He thought I'd drawn someone he knew. He couldn't place it, but he was sure he'd seen or knew this guy. That didn't shock or surprise me, but the very next week, me and Earl were up here hanging out when he came across the same picture and said, 'Don't I know this guy?' That's when I got a little freaked out."

I asked Connor why he thought the face was familiar. He answered, "Like I said, I've seen my guardian angel... this is him."

"What do you mean, your *angel*? When?"

"Listen, it's not a Biblical thing. It's spiritual. You know me and my sixth sense. I've *seen* him. The first time I saw him, I found a Bible and read the whole thing."

"You never told me that."

"It was a phase, and I forgot about the angel, at least, until yesterday." He paused. "I was about to tell you, Joel - when you were sitting on the floor sorting through those boxes, he was standing over you. You called me on it; you *knew* I was hiding something."

"You saw this guy with *me?*" I pointed at the sketch in Caroline's hand. Though I knew he wouldn't lie to me, the idea that Kevin had been drawing the spirit Connor claimed had taken an interest in me was a little upsetting. He just nodded, working one hand with the other.

"This is starting to scare me." Caroline shuddered as she handed the drawing back to Kevin.

"I draw him," Kevin said, "But I can't say I've ever seen him beyond my mind's eye. If we took this picture around the house, I'd bet everyone would say he's a familiar face. They just won't be able to place him."

"Alright," I said, "let's test that theory. Post 'em, all the pictures. And we'll see what everyone says."

While Kevin complied, Connor and I resumed our seats.

"You've got to tell me more about this vision, Connor. What else did it do?" I asked.

"Nothing more to tell."

"Well, when did you start seeing it - I mean, him." I had no reason to doubt my friend's vision or that he had a guardian angel. I knew Connor's sixth sense made him different.

"Around two years ago, when we were at the lake with Jill and Ruby." He recalled.

"Ruby? Oh *God*, Connor!" Caroline winced.

"Anyway," he continued, ignoring her pretense, "it was up there. That's weird, though, right? Nothing spectacular, just a sighting, really. He stood in the darkness just beyond our campfire, then turned and walked into the woods. Jesus, I almost got up and followed him." He stopped to mop his brow with the back of his hand. "Since then, I bet I've seen him a hundred times - but seeing him with you was different. Usually, all he's doing is walking by, staying at a distance, but now I guess he's looking out for all of us. We might all share the same angel."

It suddenly dawned on me that maybe the skunk was his way of approaching *me*. Maybe he couldn't show himself to me directly and appeared as an avatar. But why a skunk? And why *that* skunk? It was all pretty out there, but these were unreal times.

"It makes some sense, though," offered Caroline. "The idea that we all share the same guardian angel, I mean. We *are* all alive." The tears streamed down her cheeks before she knew she was even crying.

"It's alright, Caroline." I got up and approached her, knelt, and squeezed her hand.

"Why us, though?" She asked the question we'd all had on the tip of our tongues. Presently, there was no answering it.

Chapter Thirteen

Hours later, Sidney, Sonny, and Julia came to relieve us in Skylab.

"Alright, kids," I addressed the new blood enthusiastically. "Stay sharp. The rain plays tricks on the eyes and the ears." They huffed and rolled their eyes. Guard duty didn't appeal to anyone. Connor and I moved Jake to the living room while Caroline went to the kitchen to grab breakfast.

As I entered the kitchen, I found John frying up some bacon. Bread was toasting for sandwiches as Sara sliced tomatoes.

"Hi guys," Sara greeted Connor and me, winking at me. "Heard your watch was pretty exciting." A pause. "For the record, and I've already admitted this to Kevin, I know the man in his drawing too. Why? No idea." I found myself drawn to the tomatoes. I watched Sara's knife cut through their fleshy exterior, exposing the meaty center. They were a brilliant red; I couldn't help staring. It was as though I'd forgotten color until just then.

Caroline chimed in. "It's really spooking me because Gil and Seth also recognized the portrait. I still don't think I've ever seen him, and neither does John."

John turned from the frying pan where, until that moment, all of his attention was focused. "We were, uh, feeling left out of the whole guardian angel thing. Like maybe we don't belong here with the rest of you. Because, you know, we weren't *actually* supposed to come on the camping trip."

"Hey, don't think like that!" Connor interrupted. "Sonny and Sidney haven't yet admitted to recognizing the picture. Neither has Julia."

It was funny how this idea of a guardian angel had taken off. For a bunch of skeptics who a few days ago had been arguing the existence of religion around a campfire, we had grabbed onto the guardian angel with both hands, gripping his white robe as if it were the last thread of reason in an unreasonable world.

We ate silently at the kitchen table and listened to the rain fall outside. When would it stop? First the ash and now this: a paralyzing rain holding us hostage in this house. Reality hit me again, and a wave of paranoia crashed like thunder. Or was that real thunder? You're too damn sensitive, Joel, I scolded myself. Take a lesson from Earl. Learn a thing or two about keeping it all down. God, I respected that cool son of a bitch! I didn't think anyone save Connor was holding up as well. My neck craned to see around the corner and into the living room, where we'd laid Jake on one of the reclining chairs, and I wondered how he would fare.

"Have you seen Jake today, John?" I ask, ready to recite my recent story.

"No Jake sightings this morning to report." We all laughed, recalling the novelty of a 'Jake sighting' in the past. "Of course, there aren't any ditches or park benches in your house, so I wouldn't know where to look!" he added. We each chuckled again under our breath.

Speak of the devil, and he'll appear. Jake strolled into the kitchen as if on cue. Caught off guard, we went quiet, and I greeted him with a wave. He went to the fridge, pulled out a Coke, and left without a word.

Shit that made me feel like a first-class asshole, especially after the speech I'd given him about cleaning up. I could see that we were all feeling the same: ashamed.

"Sorry, Joel," John studied the crumbs on his plate.

"Not your fault, John. I'll go talk to him." I pushed my chair back.

I found Jake curled up on the floor in a corner of the family room, shaking. Coming down, I'd guessed, and too embarrassed to ask for another hit. I knelt and laid a gentle hand on his back. He wasn't responsive, but I couldn't blame him. God, I felt like shit.

Sensing the presence of someone behind us, I looked over my shoulder and saw Connor standing in the hall, staring at the air above us. His gaze was fixed, his expression indecipherable. When I questioned him with a raised brow, he slowly approached.

"Joel," he whispered, "he's back. He's with you both."

My skin crawled, and tears came in force. I buried my face in my arm. A strange feeling of calm replaced the angst and paranoia that had overcome me in the kitchen, knowing a higher power was watching us. As a soothing presence engulfed us both, even Jake's shaking ceased.

Kevin approached Connor in the hall and noticed his bizarre stance. He realized right away what was happening.

"You see him, don't you? It's the angel, isn't it?"

Connor didn't speak. At this point, the girls and John joined the group in the hall, and Kevin explained what was happening. Sara crouched next to me and kissed my face. After several minutes, Jake sat up and looked at his hands.

"Did you feel that?" he whispered. Wonder and bliss settled over his features, drying the tears and restoring color to his hollow cheeks. "It's like I shed my skin."

In a moment of fleeting clarity, I saw a changed man. I touched his arm, wanting to tell him how proud I was, and he should be. But words wouldn't come; nothing would, so I just let it go. Sara, smiling, helped me up.

The others surrounded Jake and knelt beside him, excitedly lifting him to his feet, trying to get a read on what had just happened. Jake smiled ear to ear, his chest heaving dramatically as he took deep, cleansing breaths. I knew his struggle was over. I felt that much through touch while it was happening. I felt the ecstasy of being free of the addiction that was killing him. There was much more to this angel than met the eye.

*****

Later that day in Skylab, Kevin brought me the pipe, which had been making its rounds behind me. The group had gathered here again to blow off some steam.

"Hell of a party, eh, Joel?"

I nodded and pulled deeply on the pipe. He was fidgeting, probably a side effect of the pot. "That was really something we witnessed today," he coughed. "Jake's obviously been hit pretty hard by the scene. How are you doing?"

"I'm fine, man," I tell him through tight lips, holding the smoke captive in my lungs just a little longer.

"I got a few seriously wild paintings in mind." He changed the subject, realizing he wouldn't get much more out of me. "I had this dream the other night. It was so surreal... like what's happening all around us, you know? *Surreal.*"

"Dream, huh? Do tell."

"It freaked me out when I woke up because I never remember my dreams besides the recurring face." He struggled to remember, and when it came to him, it came in quick, rambling sentences. "Yeah, it went like this: first, I saw a leg, without a foot. Next came a wing, a feathered wing, and following that was a hand... sickly looking, you know? Sickly. The background was a blue watercolor, really working into the deeper tones of the body parts." Now, he was fully reliving the dream, using gestures to demonstrate how the images would glide before him. "And some other disturbing things. Body parts, animals... a horn..." A shiver ran through me as I recalled the same dream.

"What do you think it all means?" I asked, wondering if my earlier interpretation of the dream would match his.

"It's pretty self-explanatory if you ask me."

"Let's have it."

"It's all about the struggle of man, good versus evil. The body parts are those of a man, maybe mine, and the wing isn't a bird but an angel! That makes sense, right? The horn isn't an animal's; it's the Devil's."

It made sense. But was it too much of a coincidence? Were Kevin and I repressing something we'd actually seen? And now, as people were apt to do, attempting to look for reason in the horrors of what we'd witnessed? The whole thing with the angel and Jake's transformation suddenly left a bitter taste in my mouth. Look at us morons, looking for hope in this wasteland. I reached for the pipe again but misjudged my aim and tumbled off the chair. Kevin laughed and lapsed into stoned bliss. I never did tell him we'd shared the same dream. I needed to accumulate more information before I could assemble the whole picture.

At two-thirty in the morning, I decided to call it a night. Sara followed closely behind. While alone in my bedroom, she presented me with her family Bible. Trying not to disturb the waterbed, we slid onto the rubber mattress, settling on the sheets. I wasn't in the mood for such heavy reading just then; I only wanted a solid night's sleep. "Want me to read to you?"

Not really. But I said, "Sure."

"Alright then, I'll start with something light." I think she read a chapter or a Psalm or something. Whatever it was, it served as my background music, the words melting together as I slipped into a deep, undisturbed slumber. If people needed hope, let them have it. Who knew how long it would last?

Chapter Fourteen

The days that followed that single shot of hope and enlightenment all passed in a gloomy sameness. There were no wandering vagabonds to feed or repel, and we stayed away from town as the acid rain continued its work on anything made of oil and metal. A short run to the neighboring farmhouses did little for our weakened spirits. If they weren't abandoned, they were inhabited by the dead. People I'd known my whole life. We took what provisions we could.

The big book of Sara's kept me entertained through much of the 'rainy season,' as we termed it. I read the whole thing mainly out of curiosity. The most powerful story was, as Sara and Sidney had said that night at the lake, the book of Revelation. Powerful because it was so absolute about the end of the world and a second coming. The Four Horsemen were prevalent. It was nasty imagery, too, not exactly challenging to conjure up when I was already faced with an ugly reality. But I imagined that when the Bible was written, people would have happily seen the end of the world come so they could go to paradise. It almost made me wish this 'end' would come. Were we in a limbo or something? It was written that when the world's end came, man would seek death and not find it. We were not there yet; we were still hanging on to life, but perhaps that was not far off.

The days just seemed to blend into one another. I'd lost count at day seventeen. I hadn't even realized that so many had passed until Gil showed me the calendar he'd fashioned from an old school notebook in the kitchen.

"The army isn't picking us up, are they, Joel?" he asked. I'd been asking myself the same question, but Gil looked so sad that I couldn't bring myself to distress him further.

"I'm not counting them out yet. Listen, Gil, we can't give up on ourselves, not ever." Even if doubts had crept like dark shadows into my head, there was no point in letting on. Some leader that would make.

He didn't reply; he just picked the M-16 up off the floor and walked to the sliding glass door. The view should have been serene. It should have encompassed the balcony, back deck, pool, and surrounding woods. We should have been contemplating a swim or a trip through the forest on the five-wheeler.

"Don't know how much longer I can keep it together." His voice was hollow. "I don't know. The *sadness*, everyone's sadness... I hear them, their cries in the night. The walls can't contain it. I can't listen to it anymore." He began to jerk as emotion overwhelmed him, and the tears came. "It can't go on like this, Joel. I know I can't."

I joined him at the glass door and watched the darkness distort all that I loved, all that we were. It wasn't easy to keep it together when somebody else was losing it, but I felt I had a responsibility to be strong. We stood there for God only knows how long. The sky was as the earth: muddied, wretched, and dark. You could suffer a case of vertigo from staring for too long.

Standing there, remembering all that this view once offered - the beautiful vistas in the fall, the lush greens of the summer foliage, the crisp whites of winter snow - I realized that memory was all that remained of this place. In my mind's eye, I saw the sun come out and cleanly sweep over the trees and the lawn, the field and the pool; all that I knew was there, but could no longer see through the heavy, black rain falling hard from a bitter sky, just beyond the glass.

"Did you see it?" I whispered to myself, never taking my eyes off the scene. Would the vision return? It was so short-lived. Was I shown a possible future? Or did I fall back into memory to protect myself from the present?

"What? Did you say something?" Gil's response was slow and hollow. He was only reacting to the sound of my voice, never relinquishing his stare into the abyss.

"Forget it," I answered, knowing what I'd seen was nothing more than a memory.

"There's a hole, you know?" Gil was starting to scare me. I listened as his voice took on a sobering new tone. "A huge hole...and I can't fill it, not here, not now." He stared at himself in the blackened glass as the rain snaked down its smooth surface. "No one can... such a hole, nothing to fill it." He paused, flexing his jaw muscles. "Only *pain* to feed it."

"Gil, listen, man. We're all going through the same shit here. We have to stick together. Talk to me or Seth when you're feeling down. Talk to someone. It's only been seventeen days, Gil. We've all got cabin fever. It won't last forever."

"I'll keep that in mind." He turned and headed for the basement stairs. "Thanks, Joel."

When he disappeared from view, I headed for the family room to check the guard schedule. Anything to keep from thinking as much as Gil was.

*****

Day nineteen, or close to it. I sat in Skylab with Sara, Seth, Gil, Freddy, and Sidney, watching Kevin create another dark masterpiece. Sonny, Jake, and Connor were on duty. Sonny was so stunned at Jake's recovery that he would spend endless minutes just looking at him, studying him. Jake took great pride in his sobriety. He had become someone to regard.

"So, what exactly are you painting there, Kev?" Fred asked.

"It seems so *warped*." Sara chewed her lower lip. "Your stuff's so dark."

"For me, art thrives on the dark side. The dark pieces are always stronger, don't you find? Like memories. I bet your first memory is a bad one. Mine is. Don't you find you remember those feelings best?" He stepped back from his canvas to gain a new perspective. "Even good feelings turned bad are more memorable than purely good feelings. Say you're at a park, and it's a sunny afternoon. You're loving life, sipping at your wine, sprawled out on a blanket. But then it starts to storm, and your picnic is ruined. You won't remember the sunny part, only the rain." He brushed a line of paint on the canvas. "It's the way we're wired. We can't help but be pessimists. And so, art should imitate life and be dark and sad: that way, I'm appealing to your most memories. You don't know why you like it, but you do." He stopped to drink from his juice box. "But hey, maybe that's just me!"

No. You weren't alone in that, Kevin.

*****

The anniversary of our first whole month alone in the world was anything but a celebration. It wasn't because we'd developed cabin fever or resigned ourselves to the probability that the military was not coming. No, something terrible happened that day, which would devastate the group's morale.

The fateful morning started the same as every other. We each got up at different hours, depending on our schedules in the addition. Connor and I were pulling an eight-to-noon shift with John. We met at the kitchen sink, where John poured water for tea and coffee.

"Gentlemen, ready for your coffee?" He greeted us.

Connor yawned and coughed. We'd all been inflicted with the same nasty cough due to our close confinement. He took the steaming mug John held out. "Thanks, buddy. Just what the doctor ordered."

I also accepted a cup. "Looks like we may have to hit town for some more coffee," I said, peering into the final tin. It was barely half full.

"Don't joke about it." Connor lifted his face from his mug. "All work and no coffee make Connor…"

"Alright, alright, don't go all Jack Nicholson on our asses," John admonished as he stirred sugar into his tea. "I bet we could find plenty of canned goods still untouched at the Super Store."

"Well, when it becomes necessary to venture back into town, we'll go," I stated. "But only if we absolutely have to. A tin of coffee ain't that important."

"It's important." sulked Connor.

John and I laughed, and as usual, our laughter was accompanied by deep, chesty coughs. I caught my breath. "It's not worth going into town if the rain ruins the wheels on the Caddy. Who knows when we'll need her." My dad's Cadillac had been safely stored in the garage since before our camping trip and had not sustained any damage from the rains. The tires we'd moved in from some of the cars were in good shape, but the cars were not.

On arriving in Skylab, we met Seth, Sonny, and Freddy. Their eyes looked red and tired, the result of staring blankly into the darkness for hours.

"Get me up when the rain stops," Seth said as they passed us on the way out.

"Alright, let's get settled. It should be an exciting morning!" My sarcasm was duly noted. I couldn't have known or been more embarrassed to realize just how prophetic those words would turn out to be.

Moments later, Freddy thundered up the stairs and burst into our midst, eyes the size of saucers and face a ghastly shade of white. "They're cutting him down right now," he gasped. "It's Gil. He did it, man. He's dead…"

Too shocked to speak, we followed him downstairs to the basement. Seth knelt, bent over the motionless vessel that once housed our friend. Gil's tongue protruded through his purple lips, his eyes blood red. The scene came into focus one detail at a time. The noose, which he had fashioned from a 200-pound fishing line and attached to a rafter above the ceiling tiles, cut deeply into his neck. Blood stained his T-shirt. The chair he'd launched himself from lay several feet away. Seth had cut him down with the fishing knife he kept on his person at all times.

Gil didn't want to live, not like this anyway. He'd told me that in not so many words a few days earlier as we stared out the sliding glass doors. But I told him to come to me!

His skin was pale, his expression frozen in struggle. I tried to process it. I'd just spoken to him last night! CPR wasn't an option, but Seth had rolled him onto his back and begun to apply it. There would be no bringing Gil back.

Damn it, Gil.

Seth cried, blaming himself over and over again. I knelt beside him, pulling him off Gil. "He did this, Seth... not you. This isn't your fault..."

"He said stuff, you know?" Seth struggled to speak. "He said things I should have known, I could've..."

He put Gil's head down softly and raised his to the sky. "FUCK YOU!" he screamed. Then, broken, slumped over the body. I squeezed his shoulder and stood. We left him with Gil to make his peace. We gave the others the grim news upstairs, preparing everyone for a funeral.

The girls wept openly. The guys shifted in their seats uncomfortably, cursing under their breath.

"Why did he hang himself?" Sidney asked no one in particular. "Why not use his gun? Why did he hang himself?"

"What now?" Sonny asked the question that was on everyone's mind. "What do we do now?"

"Now we wait. We wait for Seth." I turned to leave the kitchen. We could only leave the house unguarded for so long. Turning back, I added. "He'll let us know what he wants done and when."

*****

Seth finally came up from the basement later that afternoon and asked us to help him bury Gil in the back woods by the small creek where they'd first fished together.

"He'd have wanted to be by the water, where the fish are..."

Seth had carefully prepared our friend's body, wrapping it in cloth from head to toe and placing a fishing rod in its embrace. He gave a stirring, powerful eulogy, yet I can't recall a single line. I just tried to keep it together, if for no one else - for Gil.

Four of us carried Gil out the walk-out basement doors beyond the pool that was now filthy beyond repair. We almost lost footing on the slick muck that had once been a manicured lawn. Our journey to the river was short, and once sheltered by the many tree's naked crowns, the rain didn't seem so bad. Sonny, Freddy, John, and I picked up shovels and dug the grave by the river. Then Seth and Kevin lowered the body into the hot earth. Silence fell over us briefly until Seth signaled to fill in the hole. After Sara led the group in a prayer, we left.

That evening was spent in quiet contemplation as we mourned in our own way. Rest in peace, Gil. You will be missed.

Chapter Fifteen

The days that followed Gil's demise were quiet and unsettling for everyone. Nobody talked much. Much as this should already have dawned on us, we started to realize our mortality, and that was hard. We were teenagers, for Christ's sake; we shouldn't have been worried about *mortality*. Even when my dad died, I didn't think about dying. With Gil, it was different. He was our age. He had been young and healthy. And we had been there to witness it. Death of one of our own had now stared us in the face, which none of us would forget or be permitted to.

We had to get out or convince ourselves we could before the gloom and fear made someone else do something stupid. With Kevin's help, I graphed a map of the surrounding area within a ten-mile radius. The map was then mounted on the east wall of Skylab. The point was not merely to raise our spirits by suggesting a future departure; it was necessary to mark the boundaries of what we'd claimed and see what was out there, what was left. With the group gathered in the addition, I laid out a plan.

"We all want out of this house, right? I know I do. I am proposing that we do it." I pointed at the map. "Earl has had this idea from the start, and now is the time. We should begin surveying and see what's beyond our walls."

Earl took it from there. "I've been measuring the rainfall in a steel bucket for the last seven days and have noticed a considerable difference in the amount that fell the first day compared to today. Each day since I began the experiment, the water level has been decreasing. I think that soon it'll stop altogether. Then we can get out and scout the terrain."

"This is good news," I announced. "This is what we've been waiting for, real proof." I felt the group's excitement. The morale in the room hit a new high.

"Connor's going to pair up those that want to be in the survey crews," Earl continued. "We'll likely have to arrange for additional shifts up here. You don't have to be on an outside crew if you don't want to."

Everyone's hand shot up. Connor jotted each person's name in his notebook and organized them into groups of two and three. The meeting adjourned, we each poured a drink from the bar. A guitar emerged from retirement, serving as a background to our excited chatter.

Seth approached me later that evening with a disturbing piece of literature salvaged from Gil's belongings. "Don't want to bring you down, Joel," he began as he handed me a binder. "I only wanted you to see this, as, I guess, Gil had intended us all to."

Seeing my puzzled expression, he explained. "It's his suicide letter, you know? It's self-righteous garbage, justification, a conversation with himself." He twisted the top off his piss-warm beer, slammed the bottle to his lips, and swallowed as much as he could before breathing. "Talking himself into the position I found him in, hanging from the ceiling!"

"Seth, I don't know what it was that Gil could have been thinking to have done what he did, and if it says why in here, I'm not going to read it. You have to believe that there wasn't shit we could have done to prevent it, not in these conditions." I closed the journal. "We need to remember how Gil lived, not how he died." With that said, I returned the book to him and walked away.

*****

The following day heralded the first of our outdoor expeditions. We'd been fighting the mental strain of the day-to-day lockdown, fading under a black sky that concealed a forgotten sun. This was our chance to get outside and beat back the malaise. That's what killed Gil, after all, and I didn't need to read his goddamn suicide note to put it together. The stuff he thought, and the things he'd seen were shared experiences amongst the group. What he did about it was another story.

The first crew consisted of Earl, Connor, and Sidney. We sent them east to the farm where Sonny and I had found the massive Cannabis operation. Their mission was to survey the surrounding area, bring back what remained of the drug stash, and report on the farm's condition. We'd realized that the hydroponics would be perfect for growing food. The idea came to me when I was rearranging the cold room and found seed packets that never made it to the hardware store: tomatoes, lettuce, celery, a veritable vegetable garden!

Sonny was the navigator; naturally, Connor was at the wheel, and Earl sat in the back of the five-wheeler, gun poised, always prepared, a natural survivalist. It felt as though we were sending them to the moon or further. They wore layers, each holding an umbrella to protect them from the driving rain. I wished I could go with them, but there was too much to be done here. John had a flu of some kind, so I was taking his shift in Skylab.

The following hours proved as uneventful as the hundreds of hours we'd clocked in the addition since the bombs fell. But when Sonny announced their return, we sprang to life, rushing to meet them at the door.

Success! It took them two hours to return with garbage bags of the choice weed and more good news. The barn was holding its own. The interior hadn't yet been breached, keeping the operation usable for a new kind of plant.

"The hydroponics looked good." Sonny set his garbage bag on the hall floor. "We'll need some fuel, though. Their generator is dry."

"I checked it out," Earl pitched in. "It should work fine. The whole set-up is amazing, and it draws from a well."

"Eden," grinned Sonny. I smiled, too, remembering his first word upon entering the strange interior.

"Wow!" Connor exclaimed, pushing the filthy hood off his head. "I haven't seen anything like it!"

Once they were all inside, Caroline secured the door. "How is it out there?" she asked. "How's the rain?"

Earl answered. "Not too terrible. I swear it's starting to taper off. Still smells like sour milk out there, though."

The afternoon was spent on a food count and preparing the seeds to return to the barn the next day. But that night, in the kitchen, Connor came to me with a growing concern for his girlfriend's state of mind. She'd been dwelling on Gil's suicide, wondering if he hadn't had the right idea. This shocked Connor, knowing how out of character that comment was for Julia.

"She just said it so matter-of-factly, like it had been on her mind since before Gil did it. Like she'd considered it herself."

I tried to reassure him. "She's just sorting through it. You telling me you haven't thought about it? I'll tell you something, man, the thought crossed my mind. I'll bet it's crossed everyone's at one time." My mouth was dry, so I poured a glass of water from the tap. I took a sip- and promptly spit it into the sink. "Shit, I think there's something wrong with the well water!"

"Damn!" Connor groaned. "All that rain sinking into the soil had to affect the water quality sometime." He turned on the tap and poured a glass. We studied it and noticed a slight tint.

"Looks like city water," I said.

"Probably not much worse for you either." John joined us. "Let me have a taste."

Connor gave John the glass, and he took a sip. "Nope, no worse. That's pretty much what it was like the last time I lived there. We're just used to better here in the country."

"You're sure, John?" I asked.

"Hey, if it gets any uglier than that, we should worry, but for now, I'm telling you it'll do more good than harm in this environment." He opened the fridge and threw some cold meat into his mouth, followed by a soft drink. Free of his flu, he had found his appetite again.

Like cold meat, the perishables were nearing the end of their course, and soon we'd be left with canned goods, Jerky, and freeze-dried noodles. Until we got the hydroponics garden going, that is.

With John out of earshot, Connor continued where he had left off. "So, you don't think I should worry about Julia's..."

"I don't know what to tell you, Connor," I said. "Gil talked some pretty disturbing shit before he did it."

"Then I'll talk to her. Maybe she needs to talk about it some more."

"I'm sorry, I don't mean to switch off on you. I wasn't any help to Gil. But yeah, talk to her. It can't hurt. I'm going to bed- see you tomorrow."

"Sure, thanks."

Reaching my bedroom, I slowly opened the door not to wake Sara, who'd finished a shift in Skylab not long before. Collapsing on my couch, I looked at Rex, who was backlit by the alarm clock on my desk. I got comfortable and leaned into him.

"What do you say, Rex?" I whispered. "Gil's dead. Did I tell you that already? He killed himself, hung himself. Now Julia's considering it.

Connors worried. Me, I don't want to deal with it again. I don't know how I'll react if Julia does something stupid. I scare myself. If I say the wrong thing or don't say anything at all, which is worse? Which is going to push someone over the edge? Or bring them back? Probably better I say something, anything at all, but I said things to Gil, and that didn't help. Man, what do *I* know?"

"What do *you* know?" I smirked and nodded at Rex. Feeling better, as usual, when I confronted myself, I joined Sara in bed.

The skunk came to me in a dream that night, although I fell asleep with a clear head. This was the first time he'd appeared to me while I wasn't smashed. But I was vulnerable in sleep, and that was apparently enough to spark another visit. He came soon after I'd drifted off. I was amid a nightmare; I remember feeling very exposed and defenseless. I don't remember where or why, but my friends were with me. The moon was in the sky, making me pine for the days when I could sit and stare at it and the stars for hours. That moment dissolved into a scene set in a forest at the lake where we'd spent our last typical weekend. I could only imagine how it looked now. When the skunk appeared and sauntered over to me on his hind legs, I greeted him with a smile, sure now that he was my guardian.

He turned and waved for me to follow. As we walked deeper into the woods, he spoke. "You have more to do here. Live for them. Things will change, things will get better." Then he left me.

I ran after him. "Stop! Stop, damn it! I have a question! I need to ask you..."

The image of the woods intensified. I could smell the earth underfoot and feel the branches against my face as I pushed through the dense brush. Suddenly, the air turned damp and cool, and the forest floor morphed into a thick, sticky muck that stopped me in my tracks. "Damn it!" I fumed.

My shouting woke me. That wasn't unusual, as I'd roused myself before by talking in my sleep. What stunned me was that I woke up outside, in the woods behind my house. I didn't know where I was at first. I shook my head and made damn sure I was awake. Satisfied that the dream was over, and I was definitely outside, I pulled my bare feet out of a patch of deep sludge and began the short walk up the trail back to the house.

I had chased the skunk in my dream and ended up outside. Why did that happen? He'd said things would change; things would get better. What did he mean? Exiting the woods, I realized the answer was all around me. Actually, it was *no longer* all around me! The rains had stopped!

I charged toward the house, forgetting that I was visible from Skylab and might be shot if the guard on duty was paying any attention. The back sliding door was locked, so I hurried around the north side to the front where, I assumed, I'd made my escape. Sure enough, the front doors were unlocked. On entering the foyer, I slipped on the tile. Regaining my balance, I shuffled through the house, shouting triumphantly.

The group assembled at the front door. When I was sure the whole house was present, I opened the door and walked out, arms raised and grinning from ear to ear.

Their reaction was priceless. They walked tentatively out of the house, hands extended, feeling for rain. The beautiful reality struck everyone at the exact moment. We danced in the front yard like a bunch of lunatics, some screaming at the top of our lungs while others were too spellbound to speak. No one made it back to bed until the early hours of the morning. Our situation was improving, maybe in response to our bold move in venturing outdoors despite the weather. Take a little and get a little. Now there was hope, hope for something better. Perhaps now, with the burning rain gone, the rivers and soil would find a way to regenerate.

The skunk had led me to salvation when we needed it most. I no longer doubted that he was, in fact, the spirit of Connor's angel, *our* angel. I felt awful for Gil, who did not live to savor the moment.

*****

The sky was still ominous, a perpetual midnight, but without the rain, it was bearable. I kept checking the phone and satellite connections. After all, 'what if,' right? But communication with the outside world remained lost.

Mapping and marking the terrain had been completed, and we only needed to fence off our property. One afternoon, Freddy and I stood on the porch, looking at our charts and discussing them. Caroline looked on from the steps, where she had been sitting just to be outside.

"What will we use as fencing for a job that size?" she asked.

Freddy offered several possibilities. "We have access to good sources of organic fencing like driftwood and dead trees. We also found some rolls of snow fencing and barbed wire at the barn. Hey, Joel, how's the garden growing?"

"Connor's got garden duty." He was our best choice, working for a landscaping company that ran out of a greenhouse.

Caroline sighed and adjusted her bra, the only top she'd wear in the terrible heat. "Have you given any thought about going north now that we can travel again?"

"Maybe in a few weeks we'll send scouts to see what's happening, but for now, right here is where we need to be. It's getting better, and I think it's worth staying here for as long as possible."

She stretched and stood up. "Yeah, this is home. I'm going inside - see you in a bit."

Freddy's gaze turned from Caroline's breasts back to me. "You think the sun'll come out?"

"Sure, *Annie!*" We laughed. "If the rain can stop, anything's possible." I headed toward the garage, leaving Freddy to deliberate over fencing.

One of the overhead doors was open, and I found Sonny unwrapping the Cadillac. "Pretty sweet, huh?" I stated, running my hand along the classic's smooth metal surface. "My dad was the last to drive her. Sweet ride. I rode shotgun the last time."

"Are we putting her back on the street?"

"Eventually - we need to hit town soon. Connor was there with Kevin early yesterday. Last time Earl's truck is going anywhere, but they said there were still grocery stores full of food."

"Cool, sign me up for the next tour." He rolled the tarp back over the car.

"Count on it, big man!" I slapped his shoulder and then noticed movement under the car. Just as I was about to say something, I realized what it was: the skunk, my skunk. Stinky. Sonny left the garage. Kneeling, I whispered, "How long have you been here? I would have brought you something to eat if I'd known. I'll leave you some food tonight."

"Talking to yourself again?" Connor was back from the barn. "I thought we'd covered that?"

My head hits the undercarriage of the Caddy. "*Jesus*, man! Stop sneaking up on me!" I got to my feet and punched him in the arm. He faked a block. "I was just talking to the car." I slapped away his weak attempt at retribution and grinned. "Cars are people, too."

"Your dad would appreciate that." It was true: he would. "I've got some good news. The first few plants are showing growth. I think we'll be transplanting them from the nursery to the growing chambers in another two weeks." He hits me in the shoulder.

"What! That's great, man!" Giddy with success, we continued to play-fight until Connor had me in a headlock. Then we went inside and found the girls playing cards at the kitchen table with Sidney.

"Where's Jake, Joel?" Sara asked. She looked up from her hand, munching on a saltine cracker.

"I don't know. Where should he be? Is he on duty again?" I studied the schedule posted on the wall.

"No. It's just that he hasn't been around for the last... well, I think the last time I saw him was yesterday!"

"Is he not upstairs?

"No need to worry," declared Jake as he entered the kitchen. "I'm not lost. Not anymore." He smiled strangely at me as he helped himself to a slice of bread and peanut butter from the cupboard.

"Where have you been, Jake?" Julia asked.

"I was meditating in the yard, just beyond the shack. There's a spot there that's got all of the light. I'll have to show you guys. It's beautiful, really. My fortress of solitude. It could be all of ours if you'd like."

"*Light?* What light? What's he talking about, Joel?" Still uneasy around Jake despite his recent transformation, Julia turned to me.

"There's no light, Julia, there's nothing outside." I faced Jake again. "In the future, we'd like it if you could just let somebody know when you'll be out. You had the *girls* worried."

"Apologies," he said, although he sounded far from contrite. "It won't happen again."

"Well, that's that, I guess. All's well that ends well," commented Kevin. I followed him out of the kitchen and stopped him in the hallway.

"Kev, are you done those paintings yet?"

"Well, I'm sort of working on all of them simultaneously, so no, they're not done just yet." He leaned closer. "Hey, have you or Connor seen the angel again?"

I wished I could tell him we had, but the truth was that I hadn't ever really *seen* anything, and Connor would likely have told me if he'd witnessed the apparition again. I just shrugged.

"Alright. No harm in asking, right?" Kevin seemed so hyper-jittery. Maybe he had been into the pot. It's not a terrible idea, really.

*****

The following week proved productive, as we'd successfully grown the seedlings in the barn's nursery, and another trip into town netted more food and supplies. I left a bowl of water and dog food in the garage for Stinky. I cherished a solid connection to that skunk and felt obliged to support him.

Days were still virtually as dark as the nights, but a different feeling pervaded the group. We were no longer helpless, required to stay indoors and wait for *God* to fix things. No, we could try to improve our lot on our own again, which was empowering.

The family hardware store was in the town west of us, and we all agreed that the time had come to make the journey there to see what we could scavenge.

"So, who's coming?" I asked as the group gathered at the foot of the driveway.

"I'll come," volunteered Kevin, throwing his semi-automatic over his shoulder.

"Count me in!" Earl, armed to the teeth and resembling more a mercenary than a recent High School graduate, raised his fist.

"Okay, I got Kev and Earl. I have room for one more in the Caddy."

"I'd like to come. Julia and Sonny are on garden duty today, so…" Despite his offer, Connor seemed strangely apprehensive about volunteering.

"Alright, man, you sure?" He knew we were going to Mom's store. His brother had worked there, maybe even died there. "It's cool if you want to hang back, Connor."

"No, no, I want to." A pause. "I have to."

"Say no more- get in."

The drive was longer than I remembered. It never took more than twenty-five or thirty minutes, but today, with pitch darkness and slippery roads, the short trip became a marathon. This road was much more widely traveled than our route home from the lake, and we passed dozens of abandoned vehicles and one transport truck that had veered into a ditch. We witnessed mirror images of the carnage on our main street when we reached our destination. Downed lamp posts, windows blown out, blackened brick, rusted fencing; all signs of a great fire that swallowed much of its resources.

The grocery store here appeared to have been thoroughly looted, as did the army surplus outlet where Connor had acquired so many of his accessories in the past. That was alarming, so caution ruled the day. I cruised along the main drag, passing one sacked shop after another while Earl and Kevin gripped their guns and scanned the empty sidewalks and alleys. Clumps of filthy clothing concealed the dead, who looked like they'd been dragged into the streets from their homes and businesses. Some were charred, burned to discourage an imagined outbreak of some ancient plague. So, there it was —proof that others had survived the initial weeks of ash and rain. Were they still here? Were they still occupying this looted wasteland, waiting to overpower us and take what little we had? Whatever the case, we were prepared.

The storefront came into view on our approach to Maplewood Avenue. Like the other buildings on the block, it was a smashed, hollowed-out shell. My throat tightened as memories assailed me. Four months ago, Mom and Connor's brother Duncan requested my inventory count assistance. Despite my complaining, I always ended up with a clipboard, jotting down the numbers. Shit, I'd have given my left arm to be holding that clipboard right now.

I slowly pulled into the parking lot, rumbling over the downed chain-linked gate. Earl was the first to enter the premises through the fire entrance, whose battered door swung from one hinge. Kevin remained outside, standing guard while we staked out the interior.

Connor's anxiety bubbled through his otherwise calm exterior. I asked him if he wanted to stay with Kevin.

"No, Duncan's not here." He'd said it with such certainty that I took his word for it. "He didn't die here."

"Okay," I said. "Okay, let's get on with it." A slap on the shoulder offered some encouragement. We split up, covering the three aisles slowly and steadily.

"Looks as empty as the rest of this ghost town," Earl commented when we regrouped.

"Whoever was here is long gone," I added.

"Where do we hit first?" Earl looked about the store, although there appeared to be little left that we could use.

"The back room should still have seed boxes for the barn garden, and I think we'll find tools and stuff behind the counter."

Earl and I looted the central part of the store, collecting whatever batteries, cables, flashlights, and light bulbs remained. Connor slipped into the back room to gather up the seeds. We were carrying our second load to the car when I realized Connor was still in the back. Going in, I found him immersed in one of his trance-like states.

"You alright, old man?" I asked.

"Sorry. Yeah. I got stopped in the moment. Another déja-vu."

"No shit. That one lasted forever."

"I didn't let it break. I let it run its natural course." He smiled slightly. "It was... educational."

I started to feel uncomfortable and looked for an out. "Well, maybe you'll share it with me some time, but Earl's doing all the work right now, and Kevin is losing his shit out there. Let's get going." I picked up a box of seeds, and Connor followed.

Kevin complained there was too much going on for a ghost town. Shadows, newspapers, and other trash moved across the derelict parking lot because of a cool wind that had picked up from the north, pushing through the blackened trees that lined the lot's perimeter.

"Are you almost done in there?" he called. "I think we ought to go."

"Chill out, buddy," Earl chided him gently. "We've got another couple loads to bring out. Stay sharp!"

I approached with my car keys, not trusting Kevin to stay calm for much longer. "Kev, do me a favor and start up the Caddy."

"Sure!" Relieved, Kevin hopped into the driver's side and turned the engine on. Behind the wheel, he visibly relaxed. He sat there, scanning the environment, until we finished loading up. Then he yielded the driver's seat to me and joined Earl in the back.

As we passed a bank on the way home, Earl commented, "Hey, we should rob it."

"What would be the point?" replied Kevin. What indeed?

It is at this moment we first saw the flag. It would become the symbol that would again change how we lived and viewed our existence in this new world. Beyond a burnt-out gas station, it went up like a rocket in the distance. A chant arose so loudly that we could hear it over the hum of my motor. None of us could make out what they were chanting, but we recognized the flag emblem, and it scared the shit out of us.

Drawing closer, we saw they'd blocked the road with their bodies. We stared at each other, breathing heavily, the sweat of fear dotting our faces. Then I slammed my foot down on the pedal and sped through them, scattering their numbers, rivaling their bravado. If this was supposed to be an ambush, it was a pathetic attempt.

"What the hell was that!?" shouted Kevin.

"I don't know." My eyes were locked on the road ahead. "But I sure as hell wasn't going to stick around to ask."

"Those were *people*, man!" Earl exclaimed. "People!"

"What do you want to do... go back and introduce ourselves?" I asked. "Didn't you hear them and see that flag? You want to get mixed up with that?"

"No, but.... I don't know... all I know is that those were people! Shit! Just when I was starting to think that we were it! People." He fell silent, but you could see a thousand different scenarios playing themselves out in his mind. I watched through the rearview mirror as his eyes darted back and forth in their sunken sockets.

It took the remainder of the trip for the color to return to my face. I felt a little embarrassed, but *damn!* That was a shot of adrenaline. Nothing more was said. Our thoughts were our own, each of us experiencing his own scenarios. I wondered if we'd reencounter this cult. I wondered if we could stop them.

Chapter Sixteen

B
ack at the house, we explained what had happened to the group, and Kevin drew an image of the flag on the addition wall. Its wheel-shaped emblem was marked with stark yellow and black graphics.

I wondered what priorities the flag-bearers set above ours and what rules, if any, they lived by. Could they possibly be friends who mistook us for enemies? Or was it better to view them as the enemy and deal with them accordingly? What would we do if they were to show up on the property? Would we let them get that far? So far, we'd believed that violence was a failure to communicate. At least, that was my stand. Earl saw things differently but would follow my lead should things escalate to an actual encounter. Given the circumstances, adrenaline had taken over in town, and diplomacy might have been lost on them. But should we believe that they will always be hostile, or should we still assume that people are inherently good and give them the benefit of the doubt?

Give them that, and we lose our opportunity. We lose surprise, Earl would say. And he was right. That was our reality, but what does that make us? Shouldn't they be offered a chance to move on, to live? Maybe they were prepared to kill us. Maybe we shouldn't allow them a second chance. Would they have given us one? We could not hesitate for a moment: this was war.

"Joel!" Connor called to me. He was standing beside the generator, just beneath the back balcony. I had wandered into the backyard via the walk-out basement. "We've got a problem!"

"What's the problem?" I asked, knowing full well what it must be. When I arrived, he shifted aside, allowing me to view the meter.

"You see that? Fuels not going to last much longer."

"Looks like we'll have to make another trip," I said. "We knew this day was coming." Dad had designed the house with a vast underground tank, but despite our efforts to conserve the fuel, it was nearly dry. "The generator at the farm is running on empty, too, right?"

"Right. That's why I came to recheck the house supply. We can't really afford to pull any from here, though." Connor closed the gate on the generator shed and walked with me down to the garbage pit.

The facts were the facts. We needed fuel, or we'd be entirely out in the next week. The comfortable lifestyle we'd become accustomed to would disappear. With the generator, battery cells, pump, and septic tank working, this house was a bio-bubble, but without large quantities of fossil fuels, it was a dead fish, good for nothing more than keeping the elements out. Oil was no problem, but we hadn't had any use for the furnace. The septic seeped into the soil and the tank and only needed to be pumped once every five years or so. The pump and electricity worked off the generator, and the generator worked off fuel. Therefore, we needed to find a source.

I'd had the Joe's Gas and Snacks attendant fill our tank before we went to the lake. We'd have to find a station that hadn't been devastated by the fallout, and where on earth would that be? North, I thought, it would be north.

"We'll have to go north," I decided.

Connor agreed. "A couple of stations just northeast of us may have something left to offer. I don't think we ought to go west again for anything."

"I hear that. I don't want us running into the flags again unless it's on our terms. We should try Joe's first, though."

We loaded empty canisters into the Caddy, opened the garage door, and backed out, passing the vehicle graveyard that was once my front lawn. Catching Sonny on his way into the house, he climbed into the back seat, and we were on our way.

The ride into town was uneventful. The quiet of the place was eerie. We pulled into Joe's and managed to fill the Caddy's tank but feared that we had asked our last favor of 'Joe's Gas and Snacks.'

"I guess there were a few more gallons in here after all. But we are gonna need to head north." Connor struggled with the hose as he replaced the nozzle.

The lights on the Caddy fluttered as we raced across Highway thirty-three. My heart skipped at the thought that the lights might stop working. The roads were also in bad shape here, full of vehicles and debris. The asphalt itself seemed to be crumbling. Suddenly, a small dark shadow bolted in front of us, and I swerved to avoid it. In doing so, I misread the angle of a truck that jutted out onto the road ahead and had to veer so sharply that I lost control of the Caddy. Skidding past the truck, we slammed into a weakened wooden fence. The fencing stood little chance against the Cadillac and splintered into a million pieces as we passed through it. We jerked left, and the car stopped. Connor ended up on my lap, and Sonny could be heard cursing from the back.

"Christ! Sorry guys, you okay?" I asked, shoving Connor off me. "Did you see that truck?"

"Did *you?*" Sonny retorted. "Jesus, I should check my shorts!"

Connor looked back at the truck that had sent us flying and froze. "Guys, look at that - it's a fucking GAS truck."

We all got out and hurried to the tanker at the magic' G' word.

"How do we know it's full?" Connor was excited.

Sonny slammed a fist against the hull. The resulting sound was a dull thud, not a clang. "It's full," he confirmed as a smile worked across his broad face. "It's full!"

It was an absurd stroke of luck. Gas with wheels: it was ridiculous. We knew it was, but I also knew never to look a gift horse in the mouth, and that's precisely what this was.

"Let's check the cab," I suggested. "Maybe this rig's got some life in her."

Connor circled to the passenger side while Sonny peered through the driver's window. He tried the door and, finding it unlocked, disappeared into the cab. Then I heard the door on the passenger side open, and something fell out, hitting the ground with a thud. I felt a little sick at the sound.

"It's not what you think." Sonny stuck his head out the window, smiling. "Just a nasty old duffle bag with hockey equipment. Get in, I'm gonna try startin' this thing up!"

I clambered into the cab. Connor and I watched as Sonny turned the key. We heard the familiar click of a vehicle that says 'no more' about a dozen times before the payoff. A few violent thrusts of the stick and stomps on the clutch, and Sonny got it running!

"So, you *do* know trucks!" Eyeing the gears and pedals, I certainly hoped he knew.

"You're the fucking truck whisperer, man!" declared Connor, slapping the dashboard.

"Sure, I drove a thousand miles once with my dad back in the day." Sonny was proud; this was his shining moment.

"Yeah, but have you been in the driver's seat before? I think that's the relevant question here." Sonny blew him off and threw it in gear. Off we went with a jerk and a stop, jerk and stop.

"Whoa! Wait a second!" I shouted. "We can't leave the Caddy behind!" I struggled with the door as Sonny slowed the rig to a crawl and jumped out. Connor stuck his head out the window.

"I'll follow you guys there!" I shouted. Connor offered a thumbs-up as I hustled back to the Cadillac. The Caddy turned over on the first try. What a gem. I navigated it over the shattered fence, through the ditch, and back onto Route 8. Sonny was just a few yards ahead, still a bit jerky on the clutch, but we were on our way. Things were looking up. The tanker's cargo meant power for a lot longer than two months. This would be a significant morale boost for the house.

*****

"Are you kidding me?!" was Earl's response to the massive tanker.

"I know," I replied. "Can you believe it?"

His head shook back and forth; a smile pulled the thin flesh across his bony features.

Everyone wanted to know how we located such a treasure, and we told them the story.

The celebration went deep into the night. We drank our alcohol and smoked our premium bud. Our future would be written one day at a time, and one day, someone theorized, our present might resemble our past.

Chapter Seventeen

We woke up the following day with a start. Sidney's voice rang through the house with news that rocked our foundation, a foundation we'd worked so hard to build.

Our south gate had been compromised. A parade of cars, trucks, and motor homes drove slowly through our property, ignoring our barrier. Sidney had spotted them while on duty in Skylab with Sonny and Sara, pulling the four to eight a.m. shift. The entire house now assembled in the addition, peering through the windows. The candles were extinguished.

"Joel, what's our next move?" Earl asked.

"Just everyone sit tight." I paused, conscious of what weight my following few words would carry. "You all have your weapons? If just one of these cars stops, we assume the position, but until then, we do nothing." Earl sent me such a disparaging look that I repeated firmly, "We *wait*."

The next few seconds felt like a lifetime. The silence in the addition was palpable, our heartbeats audible, the tension building to a crescendo. But the cars did not stop: they passed on, moving off into the distance. We could breathe again.

"Shit, that was unreal." Seth pressed both palms hard against his eyes. Then Kevin spoke up.

"Great gates, Earl. Solid!"

He rolled his eyes. Earl lightly punched him in the shoulder as laughter diffused the anxiety that had permeated Skylab. People, regular people, maybe hundreds of them just drove right past us on a mass exodus north, like the few before them. Maybe we should too, I thought. The moment passed, and reality set in. This road hadn't seen that kind of traffic since the highway to the west of us flooded some years back.

"What do you figure: fifteen, twenty vehicles?" I asked Sidney.

"Maybe more!"

These people were either running from something or to something. North: Where were all these people getting the idea to go north? Or if they were running from a threat, then what could it be? What could frighten a group that large? These were the questions brought up at the group meeting held immediately following the sighting. Surely, the black rain we had encountered upon our return to 'civilization' had reached the north by now, and the pristine conditions of our former campsite had long since vanished. We sat in the dark for some time, discussing the turn of events, popping our heads above the window line occasionally. The reminder that other people were out there, groups of survivors like us, was intoxicating- until you realized that not everyone was following the maxim of live and let live. To know we were not alone was a gift but a curse as well.

During a break in the conversation, Caroline peered out one of the large windows that overlooked the backyard and forest. Her chest began to heave, and her hands pushed unconsciously against the glass.

"People," she whispered. Then again, louder: "People... the forest...THERE ARE PEOPLE IN THE FOREST!" She shrieked.

We sprang off the floor in unison and rushed to the west windows. Squinting into the darkness, we saw several armed figures glide through the woods approaching the pool. In Skylab, guns slid out of holsters and off shoulders. Windows were opened, and barrels were thrust through them.

"Earl, get to my parents' room!" I shouted. He'd have a prime shot there, as it had a large picture window overlooking the backyard. "Connor, go downstairs. Sonny, get to the light switch, Kevin, Seth, go with him! Sara, come with me." I took her by the arm and led her to my room, where we knelt on the couch that backed against the window overlooking the backyard. The horde was almost upon us.

"Sonny, hit the lights!" I yelled.

The spotlights snapped on and illuminated the yard. There they were, stopped like deer in headlights. I counted them quickly. Six... seven... ten.

Looked like around ten or eleven. I slid the window open and began my 'first contact' speech while they were temporarily stunned by the artificial sunlight.

"Identify yourselves!" I yelled.

No answer.

"You're in no position to…"

BANG! A gunshot cut me off. I couldn't tell you who fired first, us or them, but it took roughly two minutes to end the confrontation. Earl shouted, "They're trying to shoot out the spotlight." I aimed at a random stranger, firing his rifle wildly at the lights, and pulled the trigger. He fell, and then two of his companions fell. We had the higher ground and were shrouded in darkness.

When the shooting began, Sara shrank from the window, curling beside me and hugging my arm. I tried to shake her, as her hold interfered with my marksmanship, but she held on, terrified. Her rifle came in handy when my cartridge was spent. A shot broke through my window, screaming past my ear: it would have killed Sara had she been actively involved in the shootout.

I saw figures fall one after another. The scene was surreal. I dropped another one myself. Then, the firing stopped.

Earl stumbled into my room seconds after the silence. "No more movement," he assured me through steady, even breathes. "I think we won." A thin smile finds his lips.

He sounded as though we'd just finished a paintball game. Admittedly, the adrenaline was shooting through my veins, too, but my brain was still trying to rationalize what had happened. Why hadn't he broken yet? What was his secret? "This isn't a game, Earl! We're not *pretending!*"

He shrugged and nodded. He knew I was right, or did he?

Sara clung to my arm as the others gathered at my door. "Everyone's okay. No casualties on our end," reported Connor.

I asked the guys to go outside and perform a perimeter search to double-check our status. "Be careful. Check the bodies first. Take whatever weapons they may have. We'll bury them later."

Freddy, Sonny, John, Kevin, and Earl filed out to complete the gruesome deed; Connor, Jake, Seth, and Sidney sat with Sara, Caroline, and Julia on the couch, trying to control their post-battle trembling. "Cover their backs," I asked Seth and Sid, pointing to our team outside. "We don't know who else may be out there." Then I hurried to throw up in the bathroom.

*****

The scouts came back an hour later. They had collected some nice new guns and ammo, three crossbows, a spear, and a pair of Samurai swords. With bated breath, I waited to hear whether the dreaded flag was included in the bounty. Upon receiving a negative response, I exhaled loudly. The idea of a flag-toting clan of marauders out there upset me to no end. But for now, they weren't here. Our enemies were strangers.

Our next task was to bury the dead.

We decided to dump them into the garbage pit out back and cover them with the wet muck from the forest floor. The act was grisly but necessary. We noticed that most corpses were covered with red burns and welts on closer inspection. Sara called them radiation burns.

"They're like flash burns. I wouldn't wish these upon anybody. They must have been in constant pain." She studied one man's abrasions, trying to ignore the bullet wound in his chest.

The job done, we returned to the house and washed up in the basement bathroom. As we retired to Skylab, our minds wandered, thinking about the fight, the killing. Kevin, Sara, and Seth stood guard at the windows while the rest of us sat in the remaining chairs we'd scavenged from the dining room and opened the floor for some healing deliberation on the subject.

Emotions ran high, and tears were shed. Buried in the forest, not a hundred feet away, were the remains of eleven people we'd killed. We would reiterate to each other that we killed in self-defense to appease our fragile consciences. Some couldn't bear the weight of their actions and swore never to take up arms again.

"Listen." John took it upon himself to deliver a reality check. "It was us or them, man. Joel tried talking them down. We were left with no alternatives. They asked for it! *They* signed their lives away by firing at *us*." With each word, John became more determined. "Christ, I think I shot two of them dead myself. You think I feel *guilty* about that? You think I feel *bad* about protecting my girlfriend, this house, and my friends? Screw that, I'll do it again in a heartbeat. I look forward to it!"

Jake nodded and sipped at his water. Shit changes everyone in some way. I now believed Jake had a helping hand; that was the accepted word around the house. Being present for Jake's transition was enough to believe in a higher power.

The evening saw Sara, Kevin, and Seth finish their shift and join what had transformed into another victory party. We'd essentially accepted our decisions, who we were, and who we would have to become to stay alive. The weed made us laugh. It also made us forget.

*****

October delivered a mighty wind that blew the tops off the dead birch in the front yard and felled many more trees whose roots had long since lost their hold in the black muck. It was a stronger wind than September's, still from the north and getting cooler.

On the first Friday of the month, we celebrated Caroline's birthday. The clan gathered in the addition to enjoy a party that, for once, had nothing to do with victory over the elements or our enemies. Caroline was visibly touched by our efforts to make the day memorable for her.

"Thanks, guys," she said, standing at the north end of Skylab while we looked on. "This means a lot to me..." Then her face began to contort, thoughts of her absent family haunting her. John hugged her against his bare chest. Then he turned to us.

"A little music, Maestro...."

Sidney pushed the button on the player. We watched them dance to the gentle, haunting melody while candlelight lit their faces. It was beautiful. Our new existence was far from ideal, but it never got so bad that love failed to flourish. I reached for Sara's hand and squeezed.

I noticed the vacant stares from those in the group who hadn't entered this nightmare with a partner or had lost their partner soon after. Their loneliness was palpable. My heart went out to them.

The party skyrocketed not long after the first dance. The shifts at the windows were shortened to an hour at a time so that everyone could enjoy the evening.

My spell on duty passed quickly enough. I stumbled to bed after saying goodnight to Sara, who arrived to replace me.

I stood in my room, rubbing my eyes to ease the ache. I fell quickly into bed, my body limp with fatigue. But no sooner had I closed my eyes than they were forced open again by an awful vision. A vision so realistic that I knew I had to tell someone immediately. What was happening to me? First, the skunk, then the angel, and now this. Was I turning into Connor?

Given the circumstances, I knew better than to doubt a vision so real, so I hurried back into the addition, where everyone was slouched in their couches and armchairs. "We've got to close the gates," I said urgently.

"Right now?" Kevin looked confused.

"Yes, right now! Don't ask; let's get it done!"

Four of us moved quickly down the driveway and along the ditch that led to our recently ravaged wood and metal gates. The majority of our crew remained behind to continue watch in the addition. Moments later, we heard the soft growl of approaching vehicles and high-tailed it back to the house without accomplishing our task. Then, their headlights shone mercilessly over our sanctuary, and we were compromised.

Chapter Eighteen

We lunged for cover behind the line of cars along the front lawn.

"How'd you know, Joel?" Connor whispered as we huddled behind his old four-runner. "I mean, you couldn't have seen them."

I raised a finger to my lips as the motorcade approached. Then I glanced at Earl and John, eyes like slivers, muscles tense, anxious to spring into action.

The intruders were riding motorcycles with big, nasty-looking engines. We counted seven of them. They stopped barely ten feet from us, parked, and looked the silent house up and down. Their leather jackets, long hair, and decorated hogs identified them as bikers. One commented on this being a great new clubhouse; another wondered if any women were inside. My stomach muscles clenched, and my trigger finger twitched as I imagined our sanctuary - and our girlfriends - being exposed to the heresy of these assholes.

John sprang out first. He shoved his shotgun barrel right into an approaching biker's balls. Connor, Earl, and I appeared over the vehicle hoods, covering them all.

"Walk away, jerkoffs," I ordered. "This place belongs to us. You either walk away from here, or we take you down."

John nudged his gun, making his target wince and step back. "Your dick is going to take the bullet train to the curb, asshole!"

The other bikers glanced at each other uncertainly. We were at one of those terrible stalemates where both sides had too much to lose by giving in. Then there was a flash of movement - John's man grabbed the rifle barrel.

BOOM!!!

The stranger fell heavily onto his back, blood exploding from his crotch. Behind us, the door opened. Seth was there, framed by the interior light, aiming an M-16 at the invaders.

"Get inside, boys!" he shouted to us.

We ran for it. Seth slammed the door behind us. Seconds later, bullets thudded into the double steel doors, exploding the windows. The sentries in Skylab fired back, mowing the enemy down, while Seth, John, Connor, Earl, and I threw ourselves onto the hall floor. After minutes that felt like hours, the gunfire stopped.

"They're scattering," we heard someone yell from the addition. "Joel, they're scattering!"

We ran upstairs and into the addition, taking advantage of the ceasefire. "How many left?" I asked.

"Three - and they just booked outta here." Freddy reloaded his automatic.

Slowly, silently, weapons poised, we went back downstairs. When we opened the bullet-pocked door, we first saw the silent form of the biker that John had emasculated. The porch light flickered, making the corpse the focus of a horrific light show. Beyond him were three more bodies slumped on the grass with exploded skulls.

Seth stumbled onto the lawn and began puking. I took deep, gulping breaths to avoid following his example. That was when Earl took charge. I wasn't complaining.

"Let's take stock of these bodies and throw 'em into the pit."

Callous as his words were, they were practical. We didn't need the stink of their rot to remind us of our actions. Kevin brought a wheelbarrow from the garage, and we hefted the five bodies in, one after the other. When one guy's brains dribbled over the side, Seth puked again. Sidney helped him indoors while Earl walked ahead to the pit. We flanked the makeshift hearse as Kevin maneuvered it toward the burial site.

"My ... face.... hurts."

Kevin dropped the wheelbarrow handles and stumbled backward so quickly that he fell on his ass. "Guys, I've got a live one here!"

We all stared in disbelief. It was one of those surreal moments when you don't know what you're supposed to do. One of the bodies was moving, weakly at first, grasping at the wheelbarrow's metal edges. Then, a shape sat up straight, brushing aside the lifeless limbs of his buddies, and stumbled out onto the grass. The man's face was partially shot away, and one arm hung like a wet dish rag, but he was alive.

What should we do? Should we take out our weapons and finish this guy off? No... no, we couldn't. He had survived: he was a survivor just like us.

"Go," Kevin hissed at him. "Go, run! Get out of here!"

The biker staggered toward the field. Just then, Earl appeared from the pit, shovel over his shoulder. He took one look at the fleeing figure and yanked out his automatic. Before we could shout, he fired. Three bullets punched through the man's bare back and exited his chest in a red cloud.

"What are you doing, asshole!!" Connor yelled at Earl.

"Shooting this prick before he brought back reinforcements, what the fuck's your problem? Why'd you let him go?"

We couldn't answer. Standing in the dark, a mass grave awaiting our most recent offering, I had a sinking feeling we didn't know what was right anymore.

*****

After breakfast, I wandered around the property the following day, superficially patrolling it while trying to remember everything as it had been before the darkness and blood. During my rounds, I came upon Jake in his fortress of solitude. Sitting on the ground, gazing into the inky distance, he showed no sign of noticing me.

"Jake..." I approached him carefully. "Jake, you awake?"

"I knew you were there, Joel," he answered without moving.

I didn't know what to say to that.

Jake rose from the filthy ground in one fluid motion. "I hadn't expected you so soon. What brought you to 'the forbidden zone'?" He waggled his nimble fingers, gently mocking Earl's disdain for places outside our protected bubble.

"Just patrolling. And... remembering."

His face was the picture of empathy. "Yeah, I do that a lot."

We fell silent for a few minutes. Then, suddenly, I began to laugh. Not giggle. Not chuckle. Hysterical laughter ripped through me at a memory of us here, at the shed. Jake grinned patiently while I doubled over.

"I'm sorry," I choked. "It's just... a memory."

"I think I know the one." He pointed to the broken window and gave up a toothy smile. "What would we be without them?"

That's when Jake left us. A shot cracked behind us, and he lunged in front of me. A bullet tore into Jake's small frame, puncturing his heart. I caught him and pulled him from the shed's doorway. He groaned terribly, blood flowing freely from his chest. I struggled to stop the bleeding, but it was a losing battle. Two more shots sank into the earth next to us.

"It's supposed to be this way..." Jake whispered as blood bubbled from his mouth and nostrils.

I choked on my tears as they rushed out of my eyes and down my throat.

"Don't do that for me, Joel... not for me...."

His head was on my lap. I crouched over him, crying, frantically pushing down on the wound with my hands. "It's supposed to be like this," he kept saying.

"What? What are you saying? What are you *talking* about?" I wept.

"The angel, Joel.... He told me this would happen." Those were Jake's final words. His eyes fluttered, and his spirit departed.

Jake now lay dead on my lap. I gently lowered him to the earth, picked up his machine gun, and peered carefully around the shack doorway to scan where the shot had come from. I couldn't see anyone. I had to move to the safety of the house.

"I'll be back, Jake," I whispered. Then I sprang to my feet and ran. I hadn't run like that since the skunk last challenged me: I was fast and agile, weaving around trees and under fallen branches. Shots were fired again. I could hear some hitting the trees while others whizzed past, searching for me. The adrenaline pushed me to my absolute limit as I drew closer to the hill, closer to home. I almost didn't realize I'd been hit.

The bullet penetrated my right upper leg, causing me to stumble and fall. Grasping the wound with both hands, I got up again and struggled to the shelter of a large spruce. The shooting finally ceased, and I waited for some time, listening to my assailants' approach. They didn't pursue me, and soon, I heard the voices of my friends as they rushed through the woods, calling out my name.

Sonny found me. "What's happening? We heard shots." He scanned the surrounding forest. "Where are the shooters?"

"Gone, I think." The pain was pulsating now, interfering with my motor skills. My whole body throbbed. "I'm hit, Sonny. And Jake..."

"Jake? He's out here, too?"

"He's dead."

Sonny flinched as if struck. He scanned my pale, tear-soaked face. His chin trembled. "Where... where is he?"

"At the shed."

"We've got to get you to the house. I'll come back for Jake when we've got you safe." Sonny hoisted me over his shoulder and headed up the path. Earl and Kevin bolted down the lawn to meet us.

"Guys!" Sonny hollered. "I got Joel!!"

"What happened to him?" Earl asked.

"He's been shot... and Jake's dead."

"Dead?!" Kevin turned white. "Dead?" he repeated incredulously. Sonny just nodded. Earl said nothing, but he looked just as sick. Gripping their guns and glancing backward, they silently accompanied us to the house.

Sara met us at the back basement door. "*Oh God*, what happened to you? Were you shot?"

"He took one in the leg, Sara." Sonny laid me carefully on the floor. He bunched a corner of the area rug to create a pillow for my head.

"I'll get the first aid!" Sara was on the verge of hysterics. Connor pulled her aside.

"Don't lose it, Sara," I heard him whisper to her. "Not when he's hurt like this. You have to be stronger than that for him. He's going to be okay. He's only hit in the leg."

"That could mean a *million* things, Connor. People die from leg wounds. If he's been hit in an artery-"

"He's *not* going to die."

"I'm not ready for him to die. I – I'm not prepared for this…" She started to panic again.

"Clear your head, Sara. Think about Joel."

She took a deep breath. "Okay… okay. You get the first aid kit. I'll stay with him. Get the advanced kit, grab some towels, and have someone boil some water."

Connor disappeared up the stairs. The group stood at a concerned yet respectful distance while Sara hovered over me.

"You'll be fine, Joel." She brushed the hair from my forehead while my bloody fingers clasped hers. "Connor's getting the first aid kit. Sonny, pull his pants off."

"*Shit.* You'll owe me for this one." Sonny winked at me. The pain that seared through my body as the pants passed over the wound almost made me retch.

"Jake…" I whispered under my breath. "I'm sorry…" My eyelids flickered. I felt cold.

Sara stared at Sonny and asked him what I meant. He told her and the others about Jake. The shock of losing another friend incurred gasps and, from some, tears. Sonny refused to give in to grief.

"That's why we all must get back to our watch. Earl, I'd put people outside on the ground to listen for whoever did this." Sonny gave the command.

Earl nodded. "Joel would have wanted to keep the watch."

"*Jesus, Earl,* don't say 'Joel would have wanted.' He's not dead!" Sara's voice rose in pitch but remained calm, wiping the sweat from my brow and smiling reassuringly at me.

I could hear Earl now clearly putting a plan in place. "Anyone who can't help here, take your place at a window. Sonny- turn on the backlights, then you, John, and Sid listen for anything out back. Stay on the porch, close to the house." He knelt beside me and laid a reassuring hand on my chest. "You'll be alright, buddy."

The group scattered as Connor resurfaced with the medical kit. Sara loaded a syringe with morphine and jabbed the needle into the meat of my leg with great care and purpose. I winced. She went to work on my leg while Connor hovered nearby, ready to lend a hand if needed.

The morphine took effect immediately. I remembered finding it while scavenging for medical supplies in a downtown clinic where Sara had worked during her co-op with the high school. Thank God she had. The injection deadened the pain, but exhaustion and blood loss finally forced me to pass out.

Hours later, I awoke in my bed, groggy and in pain. I rubbed my eyes slowly but deeply, seeing stars when I opened them. When the light show cleared, I saw Sara. She was leaning over me, running her fingers gently down my face.

"I'm still here," I reassured her, smiling goofily. The morphine left me giddy.

"I'm glad." Leaning in, she kissed my forehead. "Your leg should be fine. The bullet didn't break any bones or hit an artery. It passed right through your Vastus Lateralis."

"I thought you said it went through my leg," I pouted. We both laughed. Then Sara's face changed mid-laugh from an expression of exuberant happiness to deep pain.

"What is it? What's wrong?"

"The guys picked up Jake this morning." She struggled to continue. "He's been out all night, all by himself. He - he's in the garage... in a bag..." She began to sob. The memory of Jake's death assaulted my senses, and I lost it, too. We cried awhile together. They say that a man is never gone until he is forgotten. I would see to it that Jake lived forever.

Chapter Nineteen

I managed to get out of bed in the afternoon and, with the help of a walking stick Kevin had fashioned into a cane for me, maneuver around the second floor reasonably easily. Sara refused to let me use the stairs for the time being. She wanted me to stay in bed for a few days, but that was unfathomable.

We buried Jake during that once mystical hour when afternoon transformed into evening. Connor and Sonny carried me gently down to the basement, where the shell that had been my childhood friend was laid out. He was positioned on a tarp as if asleep. A new shirt concealed the terrible chest wound. Julia, Caroline, and Earl weren't present, being on guard duty, but everyone else was there. Their solemn faces registered grief as they paid their respects to a friend who'd been suddenly restored to us, only to be taken away just as suddenly.

Kevin, Sidney, and Sara took one edge of the tarp while Seth, Freddy, and John grasped the other. The rest of us followed; they carried Jake out through the sliding glass doors of the walk-out basement. We trudged silently along the path toward a gravesite that John and Earl had prepared earlier.

As we lowered another friend into the ground, Sara said a prayer. The others repeated her words under their breath while Connor and Sonny watched the forest, guns drawn. After filling the hole with earth, we stood there in uncomfortable silence. No one wanted to be the first to leave Jake.

Suddenly, gunfire erupted. It was a single shot, but it came from within the house! Knowing that Jake would understand, we abandoned the site and hurried to the house. Caroline and Julia met us when we piled through the door, pointing at the garage.

"Earl finally did it!" Caroline exclaimed.

My heart sank. The garage! The skunk!

"Earl just went in there to check on a noise he thought he'd heard through the floor," Julia began. Then Earl appeared from the garage. With his broad grin and triumphant expression, he oozed satisfaction.

"What, Earl? What's the good news?" Connor asked.

"You'll never believe who I just took down." Earl returned his pistols to their holsters. I couldn't speak.

"Who? Did you see someone? You shot someone?" Sidney couldn't take it anymore. The suspense was killing them. Not me, though. I already knew the outcome.

"My nemesis!" he declared. Of course, he didn't realize the impact it would have on me to learn that he'd finally put down his 'white whale.' "My great and worthy enemy is dead."

He led us to the garage via the office to the main attraction. The lights went on like curtains in a theatre might rise, revealing the hidden spectacle. There he was, little Stinky, shot through the neck. I felt sick.

Unaware of my inner turmoil, the crowd congratulated Earl as they'd all heard the story of his great humiliation. Connor knew immediately that the murder floored me: all he had to do was look at me. I hobbled over to him with the assistance of my cane, took him by the arm, and walked him out of the garage.

"Remember when I told you I talked to the skunk at the lake?" I began in a whispered rant. "Remember when we were all messed up on acid, and I saw him, talked with him, and got sick? Well, *there he is!*" I pointed back toward the garage. "There he is dead. I knew he was there the whole time we've been back, Connor! I kept him alive, and this is what happens! *Jesus*, does Earl need more killing?"

"Joel, calm down." Connor's voice was sympathetic but firm. "He didn't know, man. No one did."

My voice grew louder, "I know that. But how could I have told them without…"

Connor steadied me as I faltered. Just then, Sara entered the office, wondering why I was shouting.

"It's nothing." I took her hand.

"Help me get him upstairs, will you, Sara?" Connor asked. "He's had a hell of a day."

They assisted me to my second-story bedroom. Connor left after promising me we'd talk again later. Sara thanked him for his help. Then she laid me back on the bed and removed my track pants to check my wound.

"It looks good. Clean. I'll change the bandage in the morning."

"You're the best," I told her as my head involuntarily shook. My throat seized as I struggled to speak. "Sara, what's going to happen to us?"

"What do you mean? There's nothing wrong with *us*."

"Not just you and me. I mean all of us. What's going to become of us?" I wept.

She cradled my head in her arms. Music could be heard through the house – Earl's victory party was in full swing. I choked back hate.

"Pray with me, Joel." Sara gently laid my head on the pillow. "Pray with me." She placed my hands together and wrapped hers around them. Our eyes met. I waited for her to begin.

"It's good to pray. It's the only way you'll be heard."

"You can hear me. That's all that matters."

Sara recited a familiar prayer that my mother and I had said together for several nights after Dad died. It had sustained us until we could sustain ourselves. The prayer had soothing qualities. It was beautiful, like Sara. I let myself relax. When she finished speaking, we drifted off to sleep.

*****

While I slept, I was visited by someone I had, quite frankly, never expected to see again. My skunk. Once again, he invaded my most intimate and vulnerable state, but I was happy to see him.

"Hello, Joel." he began. Light shone everywhere as he approached me, slowly morphing into a reproduction of Kevin's drawing of the angel. There were no wings or halo, just the familiar face that oozed compassion and strength.

The dream broke, and the vision left me as I awoke.

Michael E. Poeltl

Chapter Twenty

My eyes opened. As soon as they adjusted to the darkness, I glanced down at Sara, who was stirring. My sudden jolt back into the world had woken her.

"What was that, Joel?"

"Nothing," I replied. I still couldn't bring myself to tell her about my visions. I didn't want to scare or worry her. Connor - I had to talk to Connor. Pulling away from Sara, I tried getting out of bed alone. My leg wound throbbed terribly at the movement.

"Shit!" I whispered behind clenched teeth.

"Joel don't move so fast. I need to change your dressing first!" Sara sat up and grabbed the first aid kit on the nightstand. I laid back and let her work, wincing at the pain that pulsed up my thigh.

"Not much new blood," she pronounced. "Good. Means that it's healing fast."

Lying there, I felt my earlier anger and hostility dissipate. I still grieved over Jake, but the angel's visit had cushioned the pain of the skunk's loss. I harbored no ill feelings toward Earl for killing him. Not anymore, anyway.

Sara completed her work on my leg. "How is the pain? Are you coping, or do you want something for it?"

"I'm holding up."

She checked her watch and realized that her shift in Skylab would begin in twenty minutes. "I'm going to shower now and get ready for watch."

"Cool. I need to see Connor; can you send him in here if you pass him?"

"Sure." She kissed me, pulled the comforter over my legs, and departed. I shook four painkillers into my palm and swallowed them down.

Connor came in fifteen minutes later and sat on the couch. He told me he had been in the basement, getting his hair cut by Julia.

"What's on your mind, old man?" he asked.

"That's a nice haircut. I should book an appointment with your girlfriend."

"She'd be happy to do it. Cutting mine and Freddy's seems to have put a smile back on her face. She said it made her feel useful. How's your leg?"

"Fine, man, no worries." I struggled out of bed. Connor rose to help me, but I gestured for him to stay put. Grabbing my cane, I stood up and limped to the couch, where I sat beside him. "Look, I just wanted to clear up that incoherent junk I laid on you last night. I'm sorry for putting you in that position. It was unfair to lay it all on you like that."

"Don't give it a second thought. You obviously had a lot of steam to blow off."

"It was all real, Connor," I explained. "The skunk, all of it. All real."

"I realize that, Joel. You've got your visions; I've got these déja-vus." He tapped his temple. "I believe you, buddy. Maybe if I were any less screwed up than you, I wouldn't, but we both know that isn't the case."

I laughed. He laughed, too. "Man, what a pair of freaks we are."

"Yeah!" I shifted my gimp leg, displacing its weight for a moment's relief.

A feeling of nostalgia washed over me. It was beautiful but distressing, too. We were sitting here, having a carefree conversation that reminded me of when we would go to the hill, watch the boroughs spread out before us, and talk.

"Let's go back to the hill," I said suddenly.

"Sure, if you want to." But hesitation hung in his voice. I understood the view could only be that of devastation. All the same, I felt a need to return, to maybe close the book on that life, to accept this one once and for all.

"Good, let's go then." I threw on a shirt and struggled with the pants while Connor rolled a joint for the road. He and Seth helped me down the stairs. I had to relinquish the Caddy's keys to Connor, as I could not drive, and soon enough, we were off to the spot, just the two of us.

*****

Half an hour later, we were there. After Connor pulled into the same spot we'd visited four months ago, I stepped out, holding the door for support. Still half-expecting to behold the cityscape in the far distance, I was staggered by the infinite nothingness that one man's evil deed had placed in its stead. The horizon that would once glow at dusk with the distant city lights was now invisible. Small fires burned out of control in the distance, and white smoke poured from open wounds in the earth. It was an alienating sight that gave closure to a past life.

"No longer the inspiring vision it once was." Connor joined me. "I have to admit, Joel, I've been here since. Once, when heading to town for supplies, I took a detour. I screamed bloody murder when I saw all this, but the experience was good. It helped me accept that the old world is really gone."

"I don't blame you. It's something we need to see. I'm surprised I hadn't thought of it earlier."

"It's brutal. Here, you can take in the whole scope of what's happened, whatever that is... the Apocalypse?" Connor fell silent.

"I haven't got an answer for that," I admitted. "I do know this, though: it's not the end. It's the end of what was, but it's not the end of everything."

"How do you know that?"

"Because we're still here. Why would we be here if there was nothing left to accomplish? Why us? Why any of these people? Why? Christ, I'd like to know the answer to that one. Jake died because he thought he was 'supposed to,' for my good, for the good of us. He took the bullet for me. But how the hell does it benefit us that *I* survive? Who am I?"

Connor was stunned. I hadn't told anyone that Jake had thrown himself in front of the bullet meant for me.

We sat in silence for a long time. Then we heard the sound of distant cars approaching - lots of them. We hurried to the crest of the hill and looked down.

Lights seemed to explode on the road below us as a caravan of vehicles journeyed over the horizon. Each one flew a flag- the same flag we saw en route from Mom's store that day. This was the same group that had attempted to ambush us. This time, there seemed to be a lot more of them.

"Shit on that!" Connor tried in vain to count the cars. "Holy shit..."

"Let's get going. The house needs to know about this."

We climbed into the Caddy and drove home at breakneck speed, keeping our lights off so as not to alert the motorcade to our presence. Once at the house, we gathered the troops in the front yard and reported the grim news. No one panicked. We were worried, true, but we were resilient. Their greater numbers were a serious concern, but we had weapons, and if they ventured onto our land, they were setting themselves up for slaughter as far as we were concerned.

"They shouldn't be here for a few hours." I glanced back toward the road. "They were slowing down when we saw them, maybe even setting up camp. We may not see them today - we may not see them at all. Just stay sharp."

Earl and Sonny positioned themselves two miles south of the house, acting as long-range scouts. They took the four-wheeler in case it became necessary to quickly exit and alert the rest of us to imminent danger. The rest of the crew stayed in the house, stationed at the windows.

The day passed into night without further sightings. Day and night were still measured in hours. I wondered whether it would ever be separated by light and dark again. When Earl and Sonny returned, we all had a nightcap in memory of our lost companion. Jake would be remembered whether he'd considered himself worthy of that honor or not.

*****

The following morning cast a shadow over our home and lives so far-reaching and profound that things would never be the same for me.

What we'd anticipated the night before came to fruition. All sporting the flag, dozens of cars and RVs rolled to a stop, defiantly forming a line of vehicles that extended beyond our driveway. The entire house witnessed the event from the addition windows, as Kevin and Sidney had woken everyone with the news.

"Wow." Seth whistled. "This can't be good.... Can it?"

"I'm not sure, Seth," I replied, trying not to let everyone else see I was panicking. "But we don't have the luxury of optimism. Everyone keeps their guns at the ready. We still have the high ground."

It was discouraging to watch the flag bearers pour out of their vehicles onto our property. They outnumbered us at least five to one.

"Joel?" It was Sidney. "Joel, I think we should act now. It'll be our only chance. There are so many of them."

"We don't fire first and ask questions later, Sid. They may be harmless."

"They didn't seem harmless during our last encounter with them." Kevin's nerves were getting the better of him.

"Calm down, Kev." Connor had my back. "Joel's right. They'd waste us anyway you cut it. They've got the numbers."

"I'm going to start with my 'first contact' speech, like always. I don't need another scene like last time. We can't afford to snap on these guys." After checking my weapon, I cupped a palm around my mouth and shouted out the open window while keeping my head low.

"Identify yourselves! You're trespassing. We have the high ground. Identify yourselves!" Did my voice crack?

The front lights snapped on and lit the scene. "Joel, they're stopping," Earl whispered.

A middle-aged man, obviously the flag's leader, pushed to the front of the crowd and looked up at us. He wore a black robe belted at the waist, resembling a monk's habit.

"We appear before you in peace." He raised his arms and turned a full circle, showing he carried no weapons. That was hardly reassuring: the men and women behind him all clutched guns. "Our only purpose is to remove our enemies, and I hope yours."

What the hell was this guy talking about? Which enemies?

"We are on a crusade to uncover and eliminate those who support the Reaper." His smile was jagged and unnaturally long; I later saw that most of it was a facial scar. "We are not here to harm you or pillage your home. We only want proof that you and your group are not sympathizers who could carry on the devastation the Reaper began."

A shared confusion passed between us as we struggled to understand this group's purpose. I played along. "And what must we do to convince you that we do not support the Reaper's ideas?"

"We must be allowed to interview each member of your party separately. All we want to do is question them. If they are not sympathizers, they will be free to go. However, should they be found guilty, we would be compelled to remove them." He didn't clarify what he meant by *remove*. He didn't have to.

I loathed this guy on sight. I detected a sanctimonious prick who'd taken advantage of the universal chaos to seize power, dominate weaker minds, and hurt others. "Why would anyone agree with what the Reaper has done? That's ridiculous. This is a Witch hunt!"

"This is not a request. I am a tolerant man, so I'll let you decide what you will do. But at six o'clock this evening, that's eight hours, I will expect your answer."

Some members of the flag army returned to their vehicles to await our decision, while others took up positions around the house. This felt like an inquisition, a throwback to the brutality of the McCarthy trials. We debated our next move.

"Joel, do you think we'll truly have a chance at defeating those numbers?" Sara questioned the odds. So did I.

"I'm hoping to avoid it altogether," I replied. "If we can appear stronger than they are — make them think that we have the numbers - perhaps they'll leave us for weaker pastures."

Freddy looked troubled. "Won't they assume we are 'sympathizers' if we don't go along? They'll come at us."

"Shit." Sonny clenched his teeth. "He's right."

"We don't know that" Julia countered. "We can't be sure they'll attack us. I say we wait and see."

"If we wait, we'll lose any upper hand we may still have," Earl argued. "They've already trespassed onto our property and are taking positions in the trees. They're serious about this. This is what gives them purpose. If we wait and let them entrench themselves further, we could — no, make that *will* - lose everything."

"How would you propose we attack them?" asked John. "They're *everywhere*. We've already lost what little control we had."

"Maybe we should just let them ask us their questions," Caroline suggested. "If they're serious about just wanting Reaper groupies, it won't take them long to know that there aren't any among us."

"Then we'll vote," I decided.

"One thing's for sure - we'll never beat those odds in a battle. No way. There are just too many of them." Connor shook his head. Everyone except Earl nodded somberly. Therefore, the outcome of our vote wasn't a surprise: we would surrender ourselves for questioning. We could only hope that the proceedings would be fair and just.

*****

At six on the dot, the leader called up to us from the front yard. "We require an answer! Will you agree to participate freely, or do you choose otherwise?"

I opened the front door. "I will talk to you inside!" I said, gesturing. He scanned my face, saw only weariness and sincerity, and stepped past me into the house.

Viewed up close, the flag leader looked more like a visiting missionary than a potential judge, jury, and executioner. He was forty-five at most and sported a neatly trimmed beard that partially covered a heat burn across his lower face. Although he was now in our domain and technically at our mercy, he showed no fear or concern for his safety.

"This is a wise decision on your part," he told me as I led him into the kitchen. "You're the leader of this group?"

"Sure, my name is Joel. We are always ready to welcome new friends. I only hope that you feel the same."

"You have done the right thing, Joel," he assured me with a satisfied smile. Damned if that bastard wasn't getting off on this somehow. He stood at attention, thrust his chest out, and wore his robe like royalty. He clearly regarded himself as the Second Coming or better. "My name is Gareth. I am responsible for the formation of this crusade. We are on a mission to seek and eliminate Reaper sympathizers."

"So, you said. I suppose my word is not enough?"

"I'm afraid that won't do, Joel, as it has been my experience that the Reaper's adherents hide in groups such as yours. Like parasites, they seek shelter in the guise of a survivor, but meanwhile, they plot to destroy any remaining vestiges of our former civilization."

"This isn't some paranoid quest that's just as dangerous to the innocent as it is to the guilty?" This guy and his group technically had me by the balls, and we both knew it. I just wanted to clarify that he was gripping some big ones.

My accusation seemed to amuse him. "Joel, someone always has to pay for the crimes of another. Accomplices and sympathizers are as guilty as the offenders because they can carry on where they left off. Any sympathy for the Reaper's ideology is enough to make those who harbor it a danger to me, to you. The impure thoughts must end so we can be assured a future."

"That doesn't leave much room for free thought. Fear-mongering is just as poisonous to a recovering society."

"You speak well, Joel." Gareth studied me. "You, I can say with certainty, are *not* a sympathizer. Do you know how I can tell?"

I remained silent. Unperturbed, he continued. "I can tell because contempt for the Reaper flows from your very being. I see it in your eyes. I hear it in your speech. You're pure."

"I assure you; the others here are as pure as I am."

Gareth surveyed his surroundings. "I see that you power your home with fossil fuels, and I assume that the large barn facility growing fruits and vegetables is also your work. These are the marks of thoughtful people getting back on their feet regardless of the Reaper's devastation. People moving forward."

They knew about the barn. That was troubling.

"This puts you all in a very favorable light and tells us a lot about the type of leader you are." He offered his hand to me, and I took it. "We'll be staying awhile. Feel free to allow your group to mingle with mine. We are good people, and I feel you and I will be friends. I offer you support in defending your home for the duration of our stay. I'll speak with you again tomorrow."

I walked him out. When I closed the door, Connor came out of the family room, where he'd been silently listening in.

"That went well, man. I heard the whole thing."

"That was tense, that's what that was. I'm burned out. I need a drink."

We went up to the addition, where the rest of the group waited. After Connor and I poured ourselves a three-fingered gin, I filled the rest of them in on how the meeting went.

"He will want to put each of us under the 'magnifying glass.' The idea doesn't sit well with me, but I doubt he'll find us guilty of the crime he's punishing. None of you will come off as a member of the Four Horsemen if you demonstrate hatred for the Reaper when he tests you."

"So, when will we turn ourselves over to this Witch hunt?" Earl wasn't happy. None of us were, but what could we do? This was just another form of surviving. That was how we had to see it.

"Gareth says we can mingle with his company," Connor said. "I heard him tell Joel that."

"*Gareth?*" Freddy made a face. "The fuck kind of a name is that?"

"Gareth is the leader of the flags," I answered. "Just walk lightly around him; I get the distinct feeling that he's someone who could turn on you at the drop of a dime."

We would have to become comfortable with the deal we had agreed to. I only hoped it wasn't a deal with the Devil, although somehow, I knew it was.

"We're to wait for further instructions, so I can't say when the questioning will begin, but as Connor said, he told me to let you guys mingle with his people. So go for it. But while you're 'mingling,' try getting information from them. Find out where they're from and where they're going. Anything you think will be useful to us: numbers, male-to-female ratio, types of artillery. If this whole inquisition goes south on us, I want to be able to hold our own."

With that said, Sonny led the group outside, where Gareth's soldiers greeted them with open arms. Sara and I watched from Skylab as our two armies began to intermingle with trepidation. The flag bearers seemed normal and friendly enough. Maybe it would be all right after all. A sense of well-being overcame me. Then, another shiver coursed through my body.

"Oops, someone just walked over your grave!" Sara rubbed my back gently.

"As long as it isn't Gareth." My smile vanished. So did Sara's. We returned our gaze to the front lawn. "You know, he's prepared to help us defend the house for as long as they stay."

"Sounds like someone we can trust to be fair and not judge too quickly." Sara was so good, too good. She was too trusting.

"I don't know. There's that glimmer of power in his eyes: they're lit up, like Sonny's, when he realizes he's about to get into a fight. You know the one?"

She nodded.

"Power like that can be used one way or the other. Either way, he knows he's got it, which leaves us at a disadvantage." I hugged Sara with my right arm, pulling her close.

Our two factions stayed up late into the evening. Although they carried weapons (heck, so did we!), the flag bearers were less sinister than we'd initially believed. It was actually energizing and soothing for our group to talk to new people, share experiences, and commiserate over personal tragedies. Sara found common ground with a fifty-something woman who'd once practiced medicine in the city. They were led by a man possessed.

The evening ended at midnight when Gareth ordered his troops to bed by sounding one of the many horns. Our crew returned to Skylab to discuss the day's events and ponder the future.

Chapter Twenty-One

The weather changed dramatically overnight, as the northerly wind had gone from cool to cold. Our heavy coats came in handy once again. The summer was a memory; fall had come and gone, and now winter was upon us. A nuclear winter would be the joke around the house. Jokes kept you sane. Our humor may have become darker since the apocalypse, but at least we could still laugh.

Kevin played a favorite tune in the addition as he toiled over another drawing. Goosebumps broke out on my forearms as I listened. The beautiful melody floated throughout the room and reverberated off broken glass, empty bottles, and drywall. Music had become less a luxury and more necessary to break the gloom since encountering the tanker.

I opened the east windows of Skylab to allow the flag army to enjoy the music as well. They gathered on the front lawn one by one, staring up at me, listening. When I spied Gareth speedily making his way through the crowd, I waved. He gestured for me to come down, so I did.

We met on the front step, still bloodstained from our encounter with the bikers. Gareth stood on a huge stain, seemingly oblivious to the fact.

"Let's begin the process. It's time," he told me. Such a diplomat. "I want your full compliment to meet me at my trailer. I will tag and place them accordingly, to be questioned when their number is called." His tone was colder, and the crooked smile twitched under his beard. I felt broken then, no longer able to protect my group. Gareth knew it - I knew it.

"I'll let them know."

I closed the door and called for Connor when he took his leave. He appeared above me, leaning over the railing from the top floor.

"Connor, let the house know we're being called to the inquisition today!"

"Right now?"

"Right now, my friend. Everyone needs to be processed. I'll get the guys from the basement."

The flag army surrounded our house, protecting it from outside threats while we, its residents, were corralled. Gareth had kept his promise that the house was defended, so I hoped he would conduct a straightforward question-and-answer session with my friends. I had to hold on to that. But what would happen if he were to – intentionally or otherwise- find one of them guilty? Sara? What if he declared her to be a sympathizer? Or Connor, or anyone? I couldn't just let them be executed. I wouldn't!

A wave of nausea hit me as I watched my friends line up to be numbered and tagged like animals. The preliminary processing went quickly. Each member of my proud group was now itemized to Gareth's satisfaction, ready to be called upon. My blood boiled- what right did he have? But before the interrogations could begin, mass excitement broke out.

"We've got movement in the woods!" A frantic voice exclaimed over Gareth's walkie. "Lots of movement...." Gunshots sounded, followed by an ominous static.

The flag troops on front-yard duty raced to aid their companions in the woods. I ran to Skylab. From my new vantage point, I watched figures move through the forest, trying to climb the hill as they dodged trees and bullets. It was like a turkey shoot out there. Remembering the spotlight, I went back downstairs. But when my hand touched the switch, I stopped.

Who was the real threat? Did we have more to fear from this new enemy, or should I let them overrun the flags? Who was the more dangerous of the two? Neither was an outstanding choice. I made the call to help Gareth's people, as they were actively protecting the house, and turned the powerful lamps on our common foe.

The approaching horde was, in fact, a force of comparable size. I hobbled as quickly as possible to the front yard to rally my troops, numbered and tagged though they were. To my relief, Gareth was willing to let us help his "perfectly capable army" defend our home.

I gathered my friends in the front foyer. "Girls, you stay in Skylab and pick your shots from there. The rest of us are going into the thick of it. Gareth's people have no idea of how to fight on our terrain."

Sara protested, "Your leg!" But quickly realized I wasn't going to back down, so joined Julia and Caroline in the addition while the guys followed me to the garage. We exited via the back door and crouched behind the short stone fence, clutching our weapons and watching the two groups exchange fire.

Several of Gareth's men and women were dead or dying on the battlefield. Two floated in the black water of the pool. They'd been pushed back at least five yards by the horde, many of which were now shielded by the raised planters edging the woods. I signaled for my men to flank the enemy through the cornfields to the north and make our approach under cover of the forest.

"Alright," I whispered as we reassembled at the edge of the woods. "Spread out three feet from one another and choose your shots." The adrenaline rush was invigorating, helping me keep up with the group despite my injury. I waved them down and positioned myself to the extreme left of the line. We were ready.

Climbing over their dead, the invaders cautiously navigated the rough terrain. They began splitting up, leading the great bulk of what remained of their forces in our direction, likely hoping to flank the flag's men. The spotlight's beam penetrated the trees, giving us the advantage. Looking at the expressions on my friends' faces, I remembered the many games of paintball we'd enjoyed in these very woods. Each of them seemed hardened against the reality of what we were about to do. That was good. It was us or them.

"Everyone, pick the target to your right. That way, we won't be firing at the same person." Earl whispered from the far end. The message was passed down our line until it got to me.

When I saw that everyone was facing forward and guns at the ready, I eyed the enemy's approach, decided they had come close enough, and gave the command to fire.

We discharged our weapons, dropping several of the horde just a few feet from our position. Then we advanced, careful not to be caught in the crossfire of the flag army. While we waited on the enemy, anxiety over the girls in Skylab gripped me.

"Sonny, Seth, Kevin: go back and see that no one gets past the flag's troops. Join the girls!" They nodded and headed back as stealthily as they'd approached. The rest stayed with me and waited.

We were nearly trampled when three sets of legs crossed in front of our line. Seeing his opportunity, Earl tackled one around the ankles, taking him down. We ambushed the other two as well. No shots were fired. John pounded on one man's chest while Earl and I knelt on his arms. Earl watched with increasing interest, one hand covering the man's mouth. Then he blinked hard, produced his army knife, and jabbed the blade repeatedly into his target's throat. *Targets.* We had to see them as such to fight and win.

Connor had run down another man, fingers gripping his opponent's tangled hair as he pounded the target's head into the forest floor. Turning him onto his back, he let fly with a punch that ended the struggle. Earl crawled over on all fours and jabbed his knife into the unconscious man's neck to finish the job. Watching the blade slide into the meat of the neck and pull out left me stunned. Was it so easy to kill a man? So easy to die?

Freddy's target got away from him during their tussle. Sidney caught up with them first and looped a rope around their throat, securing them to a tree. Freddy then lunged, swinging his fist so ferociously that the person's neck snapped, head dangling sickeningly. The body went limp, and Sidney released his hold.

It was as if time had slowed to a trickle. I saw *everything*, witnessing a brutality none of us would have thought ourselves capable of before all hell rained down upon us. We had become soldiers, each of us, not just survivors. As I reviewed the last twenty-four hours, I recoiled at the thought of allowing an egomaniac like Gareth to decide whether we should live or die. It was preposterous. Who did he think he was - God's gunslinger? I knew what we *weren't*. Fuck him and fuck his inquisition. We would reclaim our freedom.

Connor leaned over the limp torso of his target, elbows resting on the man's still chest. Breathing heavily, he pushed off the corpse and lay flat on the forest floor, arms out, legs sprawled. Earl sat with his back braced against a tree, knife in hand, eyes fixated on the bloodied blade. John kept a watchful eye on the ledge of earth where the three men had materialized, eagerly shifting on his stomach, staring down the barrel of his rifle. Sidney searched the clothing of the target he and Freddy had taken down, looking for anything we could add to our stockpile of weapons and ammunition. Suddenly, he let out a strangled cry. "Oh, shit!"

"What, Sid?" Freddy hurried over, gesturing frantically for him to lower his voice.

"It's a *girl*, man. It's a little — a little girl! We just *killed* a little girl, Fred!" The news was upsetting, but he wouldn't shut up about it. I knew it, and so did everyone else. Soon, he would give away our position. The gunshots were loud, but he was getting louder as if he felt it necessary to challenge the noise to be heard over everything. He kept repeating that he'd killed a girl.

"Damn it, Sid! Shut the fuck up!" John hissed. "You're gonna get us all shot!"

"What did we do? What did *I* do?!" With that, he broke away from us and started running out of the protection of the forest and into the open field. I motioned to get up and drag him down, but Connor stopped me. "Let him go. He's got to get away from us."

Before I could respond, machine guns opened up on our position. We were being targeted now. Bullets ripped through the trees. Dead branches snapped and fell all around us. We hugged the ground.

"Let's fall back," I said. "We'll do better if we get to higher ground."

"Wait." It was John. "I think I saw where that fire came from."

"You're sure?"

"I'm telling you, it's just one gunner over there." He pointed toward the path. "I can get him!"

"I'll come with you." I crawled next to him, my heart pounding and my leg throbbing. "You guys cover us. We'll take this prick down!"

"Joel, your leg," Connor pointed to my pant leg, where a blood patch slowly spread.

"I'm going with him," I repeated. Connor looked worried but let it go.

"We'll lay down a line of fire to the left of you guys." Earl offered.

John and I slid over the small ledge, approaching our target. When roughly forty feet from the others, we stopped and waited for the gunner to fire again. John put his index finger to his lips and then pointed into the woods, where I presumed he'd detected our enemy's whereabouts. He then formed a gun with his other hand, followed by a quick slash to his throat. The meaning: when the gunner fires on our guys, we'll pinpoint his location and rush in. I nodded, gripping my pistol with sweaty palms, anxious for the moment to end. Seconds later, the gunner fired again.

We hurried up a small hill, following the sound, our approach muffled by the artillery. Upon reaching the top, we slid into a natural foxhole, where we found the enemy dug in. John leaped into action, stunning him with a solid punch to the back of the head. I collected the target's weapon and asked John to back off; I wanted his information first. John moved aside, but not before slapping the man across the face, reminding him of his current position in the food chain.

To our surprise, our captive twisted John's foot violently, throwing him onto his back. My trigger finger squeezed down hard. A fine red mist burst from the target's chest, covering John and me completely. The man gasped as he died, the deep holes in his torso gushing blood. John bit down on his sleeve to stifle his moans; a later examination would confirm that his ankle was broken.

We crawled back to the safety of our friends, gunfire now sparse and distant. On our final approach, I whispered loudly, "It's us. Grab John - he's got a twisted ankle."

Earl lifted John over the ledge while Freddy and Connor helped me to the top. We stayed there no longer than the brief time it took for Freddy to immobilize John's ankle by splinting it with sticks and wrapping it with one of the dead men's shirts. I checked my wound by patting my palm against the wetness of my pants. Sticky. Sore.

The shooting had stopped completely now. "Time to go back," I said. "But not to submit to Gareth's goddamned questions. What do you guys say? We fight?"

"Damn right!" Earl had never been for surrender. "Why waste all this adrenaline?"

"Agreed!" John whispered through clenched teeth.

Connor nodded. So did Fred. We were battle-hardened, living in the moment. Nothing would stand in our way. Not a broken ankle, not a damaged leg. We were a ragtag band of brothers, covered in the enemy's blood and armed to the teeth.

Chapter Twenty-Two

A rriving at Gareth's mobile home, we listened for voices, but no sound issued from within... or without, for that matter.

"Where is everyone?" Freddy wondered.

"Maybe they've moved into the house. Maybe they've got the others trapped!" Earl's mouth tightened at the thought.

"Alright, let's move to the garage," I ordered. "From there, we'll go straight up the access stairs to Skylab."

We got into the garage without being detected despite our injuries. The trek up to the addition was quiet and measured at first but gradually became louder as the wooden stairs became creaky near the top. We cringed.

"Joel?!" It was Sara. "Joel, is that you?" A long pause. "We're okay. Please let it be you."

"It's me," I answered. We climbed the remaining five stairs and discovered our team had already taken advantage of Gareth's depleted army. They'd taken significant losses, as there were no more than twenty of his followers left, and these survivors were now disarmed and disheartened.

Sara threw herself into my arms. Caroline reacted to John's injured foot, helping him to the sofa and burying her face into his drenched T-shirt. Julia kissed Connor and rested her forehead against his; tears of relief coursed down her cheeks. When we parted, Sara directed John and Caroline into the bathroom so she could treat his ankle. I approached Gareth and looked him up and down. He and his remaining people were huddled under heavy guard in the north end of Skylab.

"Is this all of them?" I asked Sonny.

"Every last one of 'em," he assured me. I couldn't help but smile. Then I turned back to Gareth and reclaimed our lives.

"We *do not* agree to participate in your Witch hunt," I informed him. "We will *not* be subjected to your questions and will *not* be bullied to join your morally bankrupt *bullshit* ideal!" My voice rose in pitch as each word drilled into Gareth's ego. I turned my back to him.

"We will not harm you, as justified as we may be. You promised to help us protect this house, and you did." I paused and turned to face them, giving my words time to sink in and make them understand who was calling the shots now. They were stunned at their loss; frankly, so was I. They'd come with over fifty people, and now only twenty remained. That was still more than our side had, but they were weaponless and exhausted and some wounded. "We will let you go and invite any of you to stay. But that invitation doesn't include *you*, Gareth. You are not to return to this house; you are *not* welcome here."

Gareth listened quietly, even meekly, at first. But when none of his followers accepted my offer to shelter them, his crooked smile returned, and the uncertainty disappeared from his eyes.

"I'll be back," he warned, ignoring the weapons trained on him. "This hostile action your group has taken will not be forgotten. I have little doubt that there is a sympathizer in your ranks. But you can still be saved, Joel. I stand by my decision that you are clean of this sin." His finger was now in my face. Sonny and Seth approached, guns ready, but I waved them off, knowing that Gareth was desperate. He was embarrassed to have lost control.

"I made a deal with the Devil once, Gareth. I did it to avoid a confrontation and play the odds that we'd all come out of your inquisition unscathed. I see you in a different light now. I see you for what you *really* are: a small man, an angry man, a man possessed. You wouldn't have been happy coming here and questioning us without having fabricated something from nothing and sacrificing one of us to satiate your sick sense of self-worth."

I must have presented a menacing sight. Dried blood caked my face and neck, dirt covered my forearms and knees, and the sticky spot on my pants revealed an older yet newly bloodied wound.

"I get it, Gareth. I do. These people latched onto you because you promised them something magical. You fed off their tragedies, tragedies we all share. Deep down, you know damn well most people would love to get the Reaper in a room for five minutes. But when someone crosses you, you declare them a sympathizer and murder them. How many innocents have you murdered? You're grasping at nothing to have a purpose. Well, I'll give you a purpose – stay alive."

My piece said; I staggered back and pointed at the stairs. Gareth's followers' dull, passive eyes were fixed on him, waiting for him to tell them what to do. They'd acted as if they hadn't heard a word I'd said.

Earl added his parting speech to the group, "A foolish faith in authority is the first enemy of truth." A quote from Einstein he later told me. Fitting.

Gareth glanced scornfully at Earl before facing me again. "I have every right to come here and order your people to prove their innocence! You have all made a grave mistake in defying us. We are not *evil* people but represent a *necessary* evil." He headed for the stairs. "Soon, we will be countless in numbers, and you will be given *no* choice then. And you *will* be judged."

The rest of his group fell into line behind him. Sonny whispered, "We don't have to just let him go like this, Joel. I'll do the fucking prick right now!"

"We won't see him again. He knows that we're stronger than he is, stronger than he'll ever be. Make sure they leave, though."

"Damn straight!" Sonny and the others walked the flag bearer's downstairs, out of the house, and into two motor homes. I watched from the window as Earl tore the flags from their masts and antennas and burned them in a pile at Gareth's feet. We'd gained a dozen vehicles and everything in them, including fuel and several more weapons and ammunition stores.

I sent Sonny and Connor to follow the flags as far as the next intersection to watch them until they disappeared. An hour later, they'd returned with the news and helped clear away the dead. The smell of blood was thick enough to almost see in the fog that had set in. The spotlight remained on as we hurried through the grisly work, but we treated it as work - and were becoming rather efficient at ignoring the lumps of flesh we dragged to the pit save the ones that moved or moaned despite their mortal wounds. When that happened, gunshots broke the darkness with flashes of orange light. I couldn't pull the trigger on these survivors, so Earl and a reluctant Kevin did that horrible task.

When she heard the shots, Sara dropped down and buried her head between her knees, hands pressed tightly against her ears. Earl went about the executions coldly, his face expressionless. He assured us he did it to end their suffering, but nonetheless, it was a chore I could not bring myself to do. Thank God he was there.

After we threw the last corpse into the pit, I sent Connor, Sonny, Seth, and Freddy to the barn to ensure that Gareth didn't show up there to steal our food and sabotage our efforts. Earl and Kevin finished up outside, tossing earth over the pile of what had once been people like us and could just as easily have been us.

*****

While looting the abandoned RVs, Sidney apologized again for his reckless actions on the battlefield. I told him not to sweat it.

"Shit, Sid," I said, ducking one of the many archways in the motor home and narrowly escaping another bump on the head. "Any one of us could have lost it over anything out there. You have to understand that she'd have killed you if the opportunity had presented itself. Christ, they weren't here to sell us vacuums. You've *got* to think like that."

"I know. But in hindsight, I can't stop thinking how you guys could have been discovered because of my-"

"Forget it, Sid. You lost it. End of story. We won, so look at it that way. You keep playing it repeatedly in your head, and you'll go nuts."

"Everything happens for a reason." He put down his pop, one of a dozen we found in the vehicle's undercarriage storage. "I haven't told you everything that happened after I bolted."

"Tell me now."

Sid smiled. "It's not a long story." He leaned against the RV's kitchen counter and began.

"Well, so, okay, *you know*, I was in a bad place. I ran until I'd cleared the woods and then turned to ensure none of you were following me. If anyone was going to get shot over it, I couldn't live with myself if it was one of you. Anyway, I stepped back, tripped on an old cornstalk, and landed on my back. So, I stayed like that for a couple of minutes. I'm thinking about the girl's face and how it just hung off her broken neck and trying to put an age to her. Joel, I..." He stopped for a minute. I could see that the memory still pained him. He collects his thoughts and continues.

"So, I rolled onto my side and looked into the backyard, and there they were, the flag army, what was left of them, huddled behind the deck." He stopped again, studying the cabinet above my head, not looking at it but rather *through* it, reliving the memory. "Then I saw the *strangest* thing."

"What, Sid? What did you see?" I leaned forward.

"I saw how the next scene would play out. I hit my head pretty hard when I fell, but somehow, I *knew* I was being guided and shown what I had to do. I saw myself move in on Gareth's people. I saw an opportunity to pull our asses out of the fire. When the gunfire had stopped, I walked over to them, grabbed the nearest one, and stuck my rifle into his ribs. Then Sonny, Seth, and Caroline came out of the basement and saw what I was doing. They raised their guns and ordered the group to drop their weapons. And every one of them did exactly what they were told. The one I was holding was Gareth!" Sidney beamed. "It was the angel, wasn't it? He guided me."

That was a story I'm glad he told me. Back in the house, I made sure Sidney relayed his experience to those not involved in the capture so they could understand, too. Seeing him bail like that in the woods was hard for us. They would respect him again, knowing his role in bringing the flags down. After a day like we'd had, a story rooted in purpose like that motivated everyone to see that our survival was no mistake.

Chapter Twenty-Three

E lation. Exhilaration. Joy. During the early morning hours after our victory over Gareth, we finally found ourselves able to discern day from night. The sun, that iridescent sphere of life, had returned.

While I hobbled through the house, frantically waking all sleepers, John and Sara remained in Skylab, watching the clouds break apart. As sunlight penetrated the grey blanket and illuminated the landscape, I realized we'd been living in black and white, like we'd been locked inside one of Kevin's chalk drawings.

We gathered on the front lawn, amazed at the combined beauty of color and light. As the soil warmed, steam rose from the earth as if exhaling, emitting a great sigh of relief. When the sun completed its climb over the horizon, the cloud holding it captive for months drifted south, exposing a brilliant blue sky.

We kept interrupting our tasks to raise our faces and hands to the sun's healing rays for the rest of the day. When it finally set, we were equally bewitched by the arrival of the moon and stars. Standing in the front yard, eyes never leaving the night sky, I picked a star....

"Reminds me of a painting." Kevin took a haul off James Bong and then passed it to me. "I don't think I've ever seen such brilliant stars."

"Is it any wonder so many civilizations worshipped them?" Caroline wiped away tears.

It was a cool, crisp evening, so blankets and pillows were collected from beds, brought outside, and suddenly we were all camping again. The night sky inspired us, lost in its vastness, once again able to see beyond our borders and reclaim our dreams. Gone was the heavy ceiling of despair that had hung over this house for months, that crushing, suffocating ceiling. Seeing those stars made me feel like I'd been granted a pardon from a life sentence. If I could see the stars, I could wish upon them again.

*****

The sunrise woke us as we slept on the dead, brown lawn. A new day had begun.

After a breakfast of brown beans and dry cereal, which we ate outdoors, a group meeting was held in the addition. Earl outlined a new mission he had proposed to me earlier, responding to the sun's return.

"We need to continue being proactive," he explained. "We need to know what, if anything, is up north. Is the military there? Are those bands of people we've seen headed in that direction alive? Have they created a community?"

I stood. "These are important questions. What if there *is* some semblance of community there? What if the government has taken those people in and sheltered them all this time? It's an information-gathering mission."

"It is a good idea," Sonny conceded. "I volunteer. We need to know."

Earl added, "Those of us who go on this mission will also take the opportunity to catch up with Gareth's group."

"That's right. We should catch up with the flag army and observe and report on any activity while keeping a safe distance. If there are others north of here, we don't want Gareth getting his claws into them and recruiting a new army."

"Should we send some of us away when we barely defeated the last attack on the house?" Julia wondered. "I mean, we wouldn't have won at all if the flag army hadn't supported us. I think it's not such a good idea."

"I'm not saying that it won't be a dangerous move on our part," I admitted. "Yes, you're right that without Gareth's help, we'd have probably been overwhelmed, but this is something we've got to do."

"It's a mistake!" Julia insisted. Her agitation grew. "It's a *mistake!*"

Before she could say more, Connor took her by the shoulders and walked her out of the addition, whispering into her ear.

Kevin spoke up. "I'm not going to say it's a *bad* idea, but I'd rather stay here and defend the house."

"Okay," I said. "It's your prerogative Kev. All of you have a choice to make."

"We don't want more than three people for this job," Earl stated. "I'm willing to be one of the goers, and Sonny says he's in. Who else?"

We scanned the group for a hand hovering above the rest and saw that Freddy's had worked its way up.

"You're sure, Freddy?" When he answered with a nod, I turned to Earl. "Get all the gear ready to go today and get some rest; you'll leave tonight."

The meeting concluded, and I went outside. Truth be told, it was difficult to be anywhere else. Sitting on a lawn chair, I checked the makeshift connection between our generator and the gas truck.

"Sorry about Julia's outburst during the meeting."

Connor caught me off-guard. I was indulging in a hoot off the pipe and coughed violently.

"Slow down, man, enjoy." he chuckled, slapping my back.

"Shit," I croaked through a tightening esophagus. Once I could speak again without choking, I asked, "What about Julia?"

"When she freaked over the plan up there. She's been brooding too much again. I thought the sun would have been enough to stop that - wishful thinking."

I breathed deeply, quieting the tickle in my chest. "Now, what's she thinking about? Not -"

"No, it's not about *suicide* anymore. It's something else, pretty serious, actually."

"Do you want to talk about it?"

"She'd kill me if she knew I was telling you." A pause as he deliberated. "Joel, she thinks she's pregnant." His head shook back and forth as though he were fighting with the idea of it.

My response almost knocked him on his ass. "That's *amazing*, Connor!" I exclaimed. "Shit! She must know that we'll be happy for her! What this could mean: new life, the *future* of the human race."

"I agree. But she keeps saying she doesn't want to bring a baby into a less-than-perfect world." Connor was becoming more and more distressed. "I really think she's going over the edge, man, *really*. You don't know what it's like at night with her now. She's a basket case. I can't talk sense into her."

"What do you want to do? How should we handle this?"

"*We* can't do anything, Joel. Nothing. I'll have to deal with it until she decides what she wants." Connor started to back up. "I just came out to apologize for her." Then he left.

Forgetting about the generator connection, I pulled out my sidearm and checked the clip. Full. Then I limped off into the woods, feeling an overwhelming need to take this news for a walk.

Ten minutes into my stroll, I found myself at the creek bed where we'd buried Gil. Stopping, I gazed down at the dirt mound. Gil would have enjoyed this day. Maybe he and I would have stuck a pair of rods in the stream and waited for the fish to return. Then I noticed something odd beside Gil's grave. It appeared as though someone - or something - had begun digging another hole to the right of his.

"That's odd," I muttered. Reaching down, I grabbed the dry earth, worked it in my fist, and then watched it crumble as dust from my open palm. "Who's this for?" The hole was no more than a foot deep but long and wide enough for a body. It felt like an omen.

"Stop thinking so much," I told myself. "It could be anything." That it could be an animal was unlikely, but nothing was impossible.

Jake's rudimentary grave was next on this grim tour. God, I couldn't have imagined the turn of events that would see two of my friends buried in my back forty. I lowered myself to the ground, wincing as my injured leg protested. When the throbbing ceased, I reached out and caressed the earth covering Jake.

"How come you knew so much, Jake?" I wished I could have asked him personally. God, did I wish. "Miss you, buddy." I took a few more moments to smooth over the dirt and left it at that. What else could I say? He was a friend who had played a much more significant role in my life than I could have imagined, and I'd never be able to repay him.

I got up carefully and moved eastward to the shack. I had to confront the memory of Jake's death. The sun hit the path intermittently through the ravaged tree-tops, and branches littered the forest floor.

The shed was still standing. I turned the corner, half expecting to see Jake sitting on his sacred ground. Coincidentally, his spot *was* getting all of the sun. I smiled: he knew so much.

*****

After supper, we all prepared the three voyageurs for their long trip. At least, we assumed it would be long. We hadn't the slightest clue just how far they'd need to travel before seeing something worth mentioning.

"Without wheels, we'll probably make about twenty kilometers a day. That'll put us near Elle Lake by Friday." Fred guessed. Though we had vehicles to spare, we agreed that sending them on foot would save gasoline and make their presence less detectable.

"We'll be fine," Sonny said as he pushed his chair back from the kitchen table. "It's all a matter of picking our battles."

"That's ironic coming from you," Earl laughed.

They'd departed with an air of confidence about them. Watching them recede from view, I'd only hoped that this angel we had created would watch over them.

Chapter Twenty-Four

Later that evening, Kevin painted a 'Last Supper' that depicted the twelve of us as Jesus and the Apostles in a parody of Da Vinci's classic masterpiece.

"I'm not sure who will represent who yet. I'd planned to do it last summer, but with all that happened, I never started it. Anyway, this is the canvas I'll use." He pulled the piece from his portfolio case and set it on his easel.

"Sounds interesting," Sara commented. "Who'll be the Christ figure, I wonder?"

"Good question," I said. "Kev?"

"Well, isn't it obvious?" he grinned.

"You?" she wondered, furrowing her brow.

"Me? No! I think it'll be the angel. I can't come up with anyone else who's that close to God except Joel."

I was embarrassed and laughed it off. Sara did not.

"You know, that's the twisted thing," she was not kidding. "You honestly picture Joel as the *Christ?*"

"Don't get all hot and bothered, Sara. I said it was going to be the angel, not Joel. It's just a painting, for fuck's sake!"

"Alright, that's enough of that." I attempted to end the conversation before it escalated into an argument.

"Look at you, Joel." Her voice cracked. "You like it, don't you? You like that your friends think of you like that."

"Easy!" Irritation crept into my voice. "Go easy, Sara. You know I haven't let any of this go to my head."

"Be sure that it doesn't." And she took her leave. Deeper within the house, a door slammed.

"She's got to let up on the whole religion thing, man." Kev still flustered, lit a cigarette, one of the thousands he and Earl had pilfered early on. "We don't know what it is we're dealing with."

"I used to think that too." I gazed out the window while I spoke. "But this angel thing, it's got me reeling."

Without even thinking, I picked up the pipe from the bar and lit a toke for myself. Kev watched in amazement, wondering whether I'd changed the rules about getting messed up on duty.

Before he could say anything, though, Sara returned for the twelve to four shift and saw the state I was in. She assisted me to my room. As she tucked me under the covers, I smiled, overwhelmed by my love for her. I'd hit a high with her at the lowest point in my life, in all our lives. I only wished that the others had what Sara and I possessed.

*****

During my pot-induced slumber, I had a dream. I was walking the grounds outside the house. I had the impression that I'd been walking for years and would continue to do so. Was I in purgatory? The wind picked up from the north, blowing my hair about my face. Looking down at my feet, I saw the trench my pacing had created.

"You are not set upon this path to walk alone, Joel." The voice came from inside my head. Was it my own?

"This burden is not yours alone," the voice explained. I suddenly realized I was talking with my angel. "Do not let an ego overwhelm your good sense." I couldn't stop walking the trench as I listened to the angel's words.

"The others know peace now. Keep your good sense about you. It won't be long."

I was still walking, but now I wept as well. "To what end? We've lost three friends to your precious path. Fuck you! You ask too much!"

I woke up staring at the ceiling, muscles rigid and fluttering. I was angry. Angry with this insane vision giving me hope. I'm angry with Sara for instilling some sense of religious fanaticism in me. Angry with myself for the pedestal I'd put myself on. Did I think I was on my way to sainthood? My spasms stopped abruptly. Putting things in perspective, I reminded myself it was just a dream. I kissed Sara, who was now draped over me and fell back into a restless slumber.

*****

It turned out that Julia was as worried for Connor as he had been for her the day before. Sitting in the backyard with me, she expressed concern over what she called Connor's late-night disappearances. I glanced discreetly at her belly, careful not to give anything away.

"What do you mean by disappearances, Julia? What's he doing, going for a piss?"

"For three hours?"

"Three hours? Have you ever thought to follow him?"

"I always decide against it. It isn't every night, maybe two or three a week. But we're going on week three."

"And you're sure he isn't getting up early for his four to eight?"

"Yes, and there's something else. When he returns, he gets back into bed with his knees and hands covered in dirt."

"Dirt?" I was stumped. "Maybe you'd better ask Connor what he's up to."

"I was hoping that you'd do that for me, Joel. I mean, we're having a hard time right now. Our relationship... please, will you ask him for me?"

"Sure, I'll find a way to ask him." I offered a reassuring smile, which she returned with one of gratitude. I watched her rise and leave, her hands gently brushing across her abdomen.

Chapter Twenty-Five

The Caddy pulled into the garage early that afternoon. Connor, Sidney, and Seth had gone on a scavenging expedition to a town fifty kilometers to the east. There, they siphoned a small amount of gasoline from the pumps and found something almost as exciting - chocolate bars! Lately, our attempts at salvaging any valuable goods from the surrounding towns had been anything but prosperous, so they acted like they'd found the Holy Grail.

"We've got chocolate bars by the dozen!" Connor beamed, lifting a garbage bag of assorted sweets above his head. My last sweet fix was a spoonful of white sugar, so I salivated. "Found 'em in a gas station vending machine."

"How were they not ruined?" Sara wondered.

"Hey, I'm not saying they resemble their former selves, but they taste like chocolate! Here!" Pulling out three misshapen bars, he bit into one and tossed the others to us.

"Was there any resistance?" I asked.

"Nothing," Seth confirmed as he hauled another bag of treats from the trunk.

"Wow, everyone's going to flip when they see these," Sara exclaimed.

"I hope so, 'cause we had to roll that vending machine over to get at them," Sidney explained that the machine had collapsed on its face, shattering the glass but concealing the contents from would-be scavengers. "Got some chips and nuts out of it too. You wouldn't believe how heavy one of those things is. No wonder people died when they fell on them!"

I gestured to Connor, indicating I needed to speak to him alone. While Sara and the guys inventoried our new stash of party snacks, Connor and I went into the backyard, out of earshot.

"What have you been doing at night?" I asked him and took another bite of my chocolate bar.

"What?" He recoiled and then frowned as though I'd just overstepped my bounds.

I persisted. "Is it you back there? You digging up that earth next to Gil's grave?" I fixed my stare on him. "Is it, man?"

Connor glared. Then he lowered his head and approached the picnic table, where he slowly sat down. I followed.

"What's wrong with me? There must be *something* wrong with me..." His jaw muscles flexed.

"Is it like a sleepwalking thing?"

"It's something like that. Or maybe I'm going crazy." He ran both hands through his hair and bit his lip.

"Don't say shit like that. You're not."

"Joel, I can't explain what's happening. It's like I'm under someone else's control. I know that doesn't make any sense, but I don't know how else to describe it."

"Like you're outside looking in?"

"No, like I'm someone else, walking a path they'd once walked. Like when I let the déja-vu run its course. Maybe that's it. Maybe it's nothing to worry about."

"Are you kidding? You could get shot walking around in the woods in the middle of the night! Then we'd have to bury you in the grave you dug yourself. That's messed up!"

"Maybe I'm digging a grave for someone else." He looked sick at the thought but also like he'd come to this conclusion already. "Maybe it's for the baby... for Julia's baby."

He caught me off guard with that one. "The baby?"

"Yeah, maybe this means that the baby won't make it to term and be a miscarriage."

It was a horrible thing to hear coming out of his mouth, but a better scenario than him dropping dead.

Slapping his shoulder, I stood up. "Come on, let's get back. We'll figure out what's going on somehow." Together, we resurfaced from our hidden position under the balcony and walked out into the sun.

During lunch, Connor drank more than he usually did. I didn't stop him: he was dealing with a lot. I limited myself to the tainted tap water, which was now bearable thanks to some flavor crystals Sara had found in the dry storage but lit a joint to accompany my sickly-sweet drink. We wondered how Earl, Sonny, and Fred were making out. Julia stated again that she thought the expedition was a bad idea. Connor looked up from his third glass of straight gin and yelled, "Why do you have to be so negative? Don't tell me it's PMS: you're pregnant, remember?"

Everyone gasped. I fought the urge to strangle my best friend. All eyes fell on Julia. Her quivering chin sank, and she blinked slowly as though trying to erase the last thirty seconds. Then she slowly laid down her fork, stood up, and left the kitchen.

I pushed down on Connor's shoulder as he started to rise. My touch was hard: he got the message. Sara also gestured for him to stay put.

"Let me, Connor." She wasn't asking permission. She pushed her chair away from the table and followed her best friend.

Silence hung over the kitchen. Then Kevin asked, "When did this happen?"

Both Connor and I shot him a look. He shut up and feigned interest in his beef jerky.

"She'll be fine, Connor," John added. "Caroline missed her period once, too, man; it doesn't always mean they're pregnant."

"Julia hasn't had hers for two months," Connor replied dully. "She is going to hate me for saying anything. She's going to *hate* me."

"She's not going to hate you, man," I insisted. I felt sorry for him. What a colossal failure. "It had to come up eventually."

"Yeah, really, Connor, what was she going to do, claim to have found a baby somewhere?"

Kevin's unique brand of sarcasm wasn't helping. Connor didn't react, though. He just stood up and went to the basement. I left him with his thoughts and stepped onto the patio with Kev and John. Kev lit a cigarette as we planted ourselves on some lawn chairs. John slipped a joint from his pocket and lit it using Kev's smoke. When he offered it to me, I took a deep toke. It had been a hell of a day.

*****

Later that night, when Kevin and I shared guard duty with Sara, she told us Julia's wrenching story. It was one of self-pity and survivor guilt. She'd wished she'd never gone camping and had died with her family. The pregnancy nourished an enormous sense of self-hate over allowing something like that to happen at all. She was adamant that she couldn't let a baby be born into a world like this.

"The way she was explaining herself - trying to justify her reasoning —was frightening," Sara said. "I think I might have talked her out of an abortion. I mean, I could try to perform it for her, but it'd be dangerous. Besides, I told her that a baby would be a beautiful addition to our group, a messenger of hope. Anyway, I think I gave her something to sleep on tonight. Connor will take it from there. I can't believe she didn't come to me with this information as soon as she knew."

"Sounds like maybe you've talked some sense into her," Kevin offered.

"Thanks," Sara said. "I hope so."

Caroline and John came in to relieve us when twelve o'clock rolled around. John was walking pretty well on his foot again. Sidney was behind them, looking too tired for someone about to begin the night shift.

"Ready for eight hours of this?" I asked, rubbing my eyes. The shifts had been extended while Sonny, Earl, and Fred were on their walkabout.

"I figure it can't be much worse than the four to eighter," John replied. "Just knowing that the sun's going to rise is enough to keep me up."

"Amen to that," stated Sidney, taking his place at the north window.

"Enjoy." Kevin, Sara, and I took our leave, never guessing what the morning would bring.

Chapter Twenty-Six

"Joel!" My eyes flickered open. I could hear the distressed voice of my best friend. "Joel."

He began to shake me. Sara woke up, too, and was the first to see the look of helplessness and horror in Connor's red-rimmed eyes.

"Oh, God," she whimpered, knowing instinctively that it had something to do with Julia. Her chin trembled, and tears streamed down her cheeks. When Connor nodded at her, confirming the worst, Sara jumped out of bed and charged out of our room.

"What is it? What's happened?" I sat up. Sara could be heard crying frantically in the spare bedroom, Connor and Julia's room. Studying the hunched figure of my best friend, I noticed blood covering the front of his shirt.

"It's Julia." He managed. When he began to sway, I scrambled out of bed, ignoring the pain in my leg, and caught him. I could see Sara across the hall through my open door, kneeling beside Julia's bed, holding her lifeless white hand. *Jesus*, there was blood everywhere!

I helped Connor onto my bed. He stayed there, gripping the blankets and pulling them over his head. Then I ran across the hall and dropped next to Sara.

Julia was dead and had been for hours, from the look of her. The metallic scent of blood was overpowering. My eyes fell to her hands, where I saw deep, vicious cuts in her wrists. The morning sun permeated the room, enhancing the contrast of red on white, red on everything.

Sara remained kneeling beside the bed, weeping into Connor's pillow as I massaged her shoulders. Glancing back into my room, I saw Connor sitting on my bed, swaying back and forth and pulling at his hair. He'd never be the same, either. Just when you think you've mastered your situation, fate throws you a curve ball. We'd come so far I thought we were actually getting a grip on this. I would never overestimate myself or my friends again.

*****

Sara stayed with Connor in our room while Kevin and I wrapped Julia in a soft yellow sheet. It was now painfully apparent who would fill the plot Connor had so diligently - albeit unconsciously - dug over so many sleepless nights. We would lower Julia's small, delicate vessel beside Gil into the plot.

During the brief funeral service, only the Lord's Prayer was recited. Words, even prayers, were powerless to soften the grief and melancholy. Connor never spoke. His chin rarely left his chest as he stared at the grave and accepted handshakes or hugs without offering any eye contact. I showed my support by sitting with him constantly being there should he wish to open up after the funeral, which he did.

A few hours later, we were seated at the edge of the backyard, overlooking the woods, the newly erected grave marker in plain view.

"How bad could it have been?" he whispered. I said nothing; I just listened. "Having a baby... how bad could it have been?" He lifted his head to look at me, eyes beseeching me for an answer.

"Connor...." I started to speak but stopped. I turned away, closing my eyes against the orange glow fading on the horizon. Nothing I could say would make any difference.

"Go back to the house, Joel," he said softly. "I want to be alone for a while."

*****

When night fell, I sat in one of the RVs out front, trying to piece together all that had happened to find a pattern or purpose. I smoked a bowl or two or three. When I was ready to reenter the world, I wandered into the house. It was late, and my direction was utterly aimless. I ended up in the basement, where I came across Kevin's gallery of the bizarre. He had moved many of his paintings here from the addition to make room during the occupation.

"What's up, Joel?" asked Kevin. I jumped slightly as he materialized from the darkness like an apparition. My nerves were shot.

"Nothing, man. Can't sleep," I stated. Eyes traveling over his art, I asked, "Aren't you working anymore on this one?"

I pointed to the multi-canvas piece that captured one of my earlier dreams; one Kevin had shared. It was titled 'Body Parts' and featured a torso, wing, arm, horn, and other pieces of anatomy.

"I'll be honest with you, Joel; I can't seem to find any inspiration in much of anything these days. The one thing that inspired me the most has let me down. I want to see the angel! I want to talk to him; I want more than what he's willing to give me." He scratched his face vigorously, suggesting that he'd been into something.

"Yeah, but be careful what you wish for, Kev."

I was thirsty, so I went to the bar at the south end of the basement. Picking up a glass and blowing it free of dust and cobwebs, I poured the rust-colored water. "Seriously, Kev, you should be proud of the role you've played in this. He gave you that face to draw, the one we all recognized. That face built the theory we exist around. That's *real*."

"Like I said before: real to *you*, to Connor and Jake well, not Jake anymore, but how is he real to *me*? Real means more than just a dream. Christ, since when did dreams or visions define reality?" Kevin sat on one of the stools.

"Don't forget Sid's story," I reminded him. "Remember, he'd been given a vision just before he approached Gareth. That was a gift. That's real."

"I suppose." He paused. "Or plain old adrenaline." Kev moved back toward his painter's box and fumbled with a baggie. "You feel like getting high?"

I was. But yes, I did.

*****

Thankfully, we slept like the dead or may have fallen to our deaths. After burning enough pot to drop a Rhino, Kev and I climbed atop the roof, directly above the addition, and stretched out. We were discovered by Sidney and Seth, who'd been looking for us all morning and checked that spot as a last resort.

"I gotta ask... why?" Seth exchanged amused glances with Sid after I opened my eyes. "You two look like shit."

"Why are we on the roof?" I wondered aloud, temporarily forgetting. The sun's rays felt like lasers boring into my eyes. Sidney took pity on me and handed me his sunglasses.

"That's what we'd like to know," Sid smirked.

Kevin awoke then. When he realized where he was, he pressed his body against the shingles: He was petrified of heights. "Shit! How did you get me up here?"

Needless to say, we had a hell of a time getting him down. A hit off James Bong settled his nerves enough that he could crawl to the antenna secured to the side of the house: the only way up or down.

Kevin and I apologized profusely for causing any alarm. We were all on edge after Julia's death, and what Kev and I did was our way of blowing off some steam. Regardless, we felt terrible that we were the cause of such a fierce search effort, especially in light of current events.

Connor was melancholy but assured us he was managing and didn't need our constant smothering. I would respect that. When I invited him to join Sidney and me on a property patrol, he nodded.

It was a grey afternoon, and grey seemed appropriate when we came upon the fresh earth that covered our Julia. Sid and I hung back as Connor knelt before the mound. Resting his hands upon the lifted soil as if he were touching her again, he moved from its center to the outer edges, dragging his fingers slowly across where I imagined her waist was. He placed his forehead against the earth. After a moment, he stood, wiping away the trace dirt on his brow.

As we were about to continue our walk, I spotted something that froze the blood in my veins.

Another grave had been started.

Grabbing Connor's arm, I pointed it out. Sid, who was a few paces ahead, turned around, but I motioned for him to stay put. "Did you do this, Connor?" I whispered, praying that he'd deny it.

"I found dirt in my fingernails this morning." He went pale.

"Go to the shed, Sid," I called. "See if we caught anything in that trap Earl left there and report back to the house.

"Sure thing, Joel." Sid was confused but didn't question. He checked his weapon and hustled the rest of the way.

I tried to reassure Connor. "Maybe it's just a routine now and doesn't mean anything."

He shook his head. "*No*, that isn't it, Joel. Haven't you seen enough to know? Haven't you *experienced* enough?" He paused and then turned to look me directly in the eye. "This one's for me." His eyes fluttered, and I think he might have almost fainted. That seemed strange.

He backed up, slid down a tree trunk, and broke into tears. The thought of losing him crushed me, causing me to collapse next to him. I was so tired, so drained. Crawling over to my friend, I, too, sought support from the tree's failing strength, but in doing so, the weak trunk crashed to earth, taking us both with it. The shock on my face made Connor laugh despite his distress. I followed. Surrendering control over our overtaxed emotions, we sprawled on the ground and howled until the tears returned. We were still at it when Sidney rejoined us.

"What is it, guys? What's happened?"

"Sorry, Sid," I got up. Connor, sitting cross-legged in the dirt, wiped his eyes.

"What's going on?" He was genuinely concerned. "Were you guys – laughing… or crying?"

"What's the difference?" I helped Connor to his feet and threw an arm around each of them. "Did we catch anything?"

"No."

As we returned to the house, I silently appealed to the angel: Please, let Connor be wrong.

*****

A week later, I cornered Connor to have it out over Julia's death once and for all. He was still refusing to talk about it, and I worried that his cool veneer could explode at any moment. I approached him as he sat at the bar in the basement with guitar in hand, bent over and holding it as if it were a child.

"Connor, let's talk."

He swung around on his stool and placed the guitar at his feet. "What's on your mind?"

I pulled up a stool next to him and sat. "You, that's what. Are you *really* okay, or do I need to sic Sara on you?"

He had to smile at that. "I'm alright, Joel. Seriously."

"Connor, she was your *girlfriend*. You must miss her." Either he was lying or a lot colder than I would have guessed.

"I'm still shattered that she took her own life. No one deserves to be that unhappy. But the fact is, I never loved her like you love Sara." He smiled sadly. "There was potential at first, sure, but over time, she became so depressed and moody that I lost interest. I would have left her for sure if we were back in the old world."

"But you didn't think you should in this one."

"Right. I mean, Jesus, what if she cut herself after I had split from her? Then, it would have been my fault. But I stuck it out and gave her plenty of reasons to live. The baby was number one. Shit, I could have been a father, Joel. That's the thing that's messing me up the most."

"Really? Never saw you as the type."

"Me neither." He looked up at me, and an uncomfortable smile appeared.

I stood again and picked up his guitar. "Play me something loud- all this easy listening you've been pumping out isn't doing anyone any good."

He grinned and took the guitar from me. I squeezed his shoulder as I left through the back sliding doors.

Chapter Twenty-Seven

Eight days after they'd set off searching for what lay to the north, Earl, Sonny, and Fred had returned to the house with much to tell. When they learned of Julia's death, there was a moment of silence, followed by condolences. Then, while we all grouped in Skylab, they told us what they'd seen.

"Beyond our position, there isn't much in the way of people. Not living, anyway," Earl began.

Fred spoke next, shuddering as he did so. "It was like a mass grave, but no one had taken the time to bury the bodies."

"The military.... We think they did it." Earl said solemnly. "At least, that was the conclusion we came to. There were too many of them to explain it any other way."

"It stunk..." Sonny stared out the north window. "I mean, it was worse than the pit out back. This was *awful.*"

"How many?" I asked.

"Aw fuck, Joel. A lot, man." Earl took a seat. "So that was the first thing we encountered: the killing fields. That was two days into the journey. We decided not to go any further. Who knows if we'd suffer the same fate? Whoever did that was cold, man, and a force to be reckoned with, obviously."

"A good idea. Probably saved your asses." Seth said.

"Yeah, so we decided to veer off to the east, and who do we see? None other than Gareth and his flag cronies." Earl waited for a reaction, which he quickly got. Everyone looked alarmed. Satisfied, he continued, "Not that we actually ran into them, but we did come across them camping out in a clearing. So, we set up just a few yards outside their encampment, close enough to watch them but far enough away to go unnoticed."

"That's fantastic!" I exclaimed. "Then you managed to get more information on them?"

"Better than that!" Freddy said. "We camped out at that spot for three days."

"They're no better off," Earl went on. "Still no larger than the twenty or so we sent packing, but they seemed to know more about what's going on up north than we did. Let me tell you something: the bodies up there stretch the length of a football field along an open area that was once a farmer's field. No one else could have wiped out that many people. It could *only* have been the military."

"What do you think the military had up there?" asked Sidney.

"Whatever it was, we'll never know, trust me on that. No one in Gareth's group seemed to have any idea either." Sonny's attention did not waver from his view out the north window. I could tell he was harboring ugly memories of what he'd seen.

"Anyway, the flags didn't look good at all. Pale, malnourished! Heard them talking about ripping us off at the barn, but nothing ever came of it."

Sonny grunted. "Wouldn't have let it."

"So, they looked pretty tired, then?" I asked.

"They're finished, Joel. Even Gareth isn't talking much."

"And some of them are disillusioned with their 'leader,'" Freddy said. "More than one of them questioned the way he handled us. Two of them actually went as far as to question his motives. I think what you said to them on their way out brought that on."

"Perfect!"

"So, these two 'mutineers' got to talking one night, and there we were in the ditch just beyond the fray, taking it all in," Earl spoke slowly now, reliving the experience. "We think it was a husband-and-wife team. We listened as they conspired, but we didn't interfere with the natural course of things. Then, when the dissenters approached the group, we crawled forward, shadowing them, hoping to witness a full-on rebellion."

"So, what happened?!" Sidney was on the edge of his seat. We were all hanging on Earl's next words.

"When they spoke out, they were shot in the head." Earl's hand had formed a gun, and he bounced a finger off an unsuspecting Freddy's temple. "Swift justice. Gareth's rule is not open for challenge."

"Where did they get the guns?" Sara wondered. She winced, and I couldn't blame her. It was an ugly story.

"They likely had a few stashed in one of the vehicles we let them leave with. It was a shock to us, too. We hadn't seen them with any firepower until that moment. We backed off, and that's when we started home."

"Good work, guys." That was a considerable amount of information for an eight-day trip. Connor brought each of them a drink of gin and flat pop that we'd been saving in the cold room for just such an occasion. I could see that some were disheartened by the announcement that the north was lost and the military, should they come for us, would likely kill us, too.

Their safe return prompted us to indulge. Connor got drunk again, but who could blame him? I lit the pipe. Earl, Freddy, and Sonny split up and answered additional questions concerning their trip. Seth perched on the arm of my easy chair, and I passed the pipe to him.

"Hey Seth, what's your take on déja-vu?"

"Déja – who?" he answered. When I started to explain, he stopped me. "I'm just messin' with ya, Joel. Based on something my spiritual coach had said, I've had a theory about it for a while. It made sense then, and it makes sense now."

"What was it?" I sat a little higher in the chair.

"He said déja-vu is the universe's way of telling a person that they're on the right track. If you feel like you're reliving something, it's because your life is going to plan."

I pondered his words. Before I could ask another question, Seth noticed his empty glass and went off for a refill. That was fine with me. I was exhausted from the day, and after a couple more hauls off the pipe, I was ready to give my brain a rest.

Chapter Twenty-Eight

Sara spent much of her free time in the barn now, helping tend and harvest the plants. It made her feel useful, she said. I was on my way to visit her when I heard Seth yelling something from the house. Changing course, I hurried back inside.

"What's up, Seth?"

"We've got three travelers at the end of the driveway." He pushed the curtains back so that I could see.

They seemed harmless. There were no obvious signs of weapons. If they had any, they were well concealed. I decided to dispense with my usual 'first contact' speech and allowed them to approach the house. We watched as they rang the doorbell, a courtesy that was almost comical – to the bell's credit - it worked. They stood patiently, hunched over and wearing little more than rags. Doubting they posed any threat; I nodded to Seth and unlocked the door. John and Kevin stood at the top of the stairs; weapons ready in case my judgment was off.

I swung the door open, pistol in hand. Seth stood beside me, gun at the ready. Our show of force seemed to frighten the arrivals. Raising their hands, they took a step back. All three were unkempt and had not seen the inside of a shower since the last missile had landed some seven months ago. They had clearly not been blessed with a roof over their heads, so I decided to hear them out and help if possible. I watched as Seth's expression softened with pity.

"Can we help you?" I asked.

"Sorry." A heavily bearded man who was sunburned where his hair had fallen out stepped forward. "Didn't mean to overstep, ringing your doorbell like that. We're just so thirsty, and the water is toxic everywhere."

"Water is all you want?" I asked them. They nodded meekly, so I waved them in and motioned Seth to get them some from the tap.

"We appreciate this." The bearded one spoke again. The others just bobbed their heads. Sweet Jesus, they stank of every kind of stink imaginable, but the smell of rot was the most troubling.

When Seth brought the water, they drank it down eagerly. "Thank you so much," the spokesman said gratefully, handing back the glasses.

"Set them up with one of the four-gallon jugs from the tap, Seth." I felt charitable. "You don't need to leave here thirsty. Where are you heading?"

"We've heard others talk about a place to the north. A safe haven. Is this that place?"

I hated to disillusion them, but I had to. "No. But I don't recommend you keep going north. We've just had a group return from the north, more a killing field than a haven."

He flinched at my news. His upper lip quivered and lifted, revealing a blackened tongue and teeth. I felt like I'd just driven the final nail in his coffin with my comment.

Then suddenly, the man's eyes widened and gleamed. The water jug Seth gave them fell to the floor, distracting us for the split second they needed to pull guns from their layered rags.

John's tell-tale rat-a-tat-tat from his automatic sent a bullet into the shoulder of one of the intruders and five or six more into the door and floor tile. Blood splattered across the front door, and everyone scattered. The three strangers, one dripping blood, ducked behind the wall that separated the dining room from the front hall. I swung into the kitchen while Seth took the living room. Connor came from the back balcony through the kitchen's sliding doors on all fours.

"What's going on?" Connor whispered.

"We've got three unknowns in the dining room with weapons," I replied. "John wounded one."

"Just three of them?"

"Yeah." I checked the clip in my pistol and replaced it, satisfied I had enough bullets. Keeping flush with the kitchen cupboard, I twisted around the corner to see what I could.

Upstairs, John could be heard ordering Sidney to keep Caroline in the addition while Kevin slid on his belly down the carpeted stairs, pressed himself against the hall tile, and trained his gun on the dining room entrance.

My heart pounded madly as I waited for something to happen. I saw Kevin sprawled on the hall floor; barrel raised to meet the enemy. Beads of sweat trickled down his forehead, but he fought the urge to wipe them away. Despite his broken ankle, John slid down the staircase as well, ending up beside Kevin, who motioned for him to be silent. He looked from Kevin to me and winked.

Fifteen minutes had passed, and no one had made a sound. We kept watch on the entrances to the dining room while Caroline and Sid remained in Skylab, waiting. But at some point, Caroline lost her patience. Dodging Sidney's grasp, she hurried down the hall, looking for John. When she saw John lying on his stomach beside Kevin, she whispered frantically, "John? Are you alright?"

John didn't dare answer or wave her off. He had played the waiting game like the rest of us in the woods when we'd had paintball tournaments. Distraught at his failure to respond, she began to descend the stairs, each step advising the enemy that someone was advancing on their position. Finally John jumped up without a sound and limped to the stairs, grabbing Caroline's leg and pulling her down against the steps.

Suddenly, the three intruders left their cover and bolted for the front door. One turned and fired. A bullet caught John in the back, and he slumped onto the stairs, blood pumping from the wound. Kevin opened up from the floor and hit the shooter in the chest and face, dropping him like a rag doll. The other two retreated into the dining room.

Kevin continued firing at the wall separating the two rooms, hoping his blind aim might cut them down. When his ammunition ran out, he scrambled over to John, who was lying across a hysterical Caroline's lap. While Caroline trailed behind, he hauled John's limp form up the remaining steps to the second floor.

Connor and I opened up on the wall while Kevin raced up the stairs. Seth joined in from the office on the other side of the hall. We could hear the windows smashing on the outside walls as our bullets punched through. Encouraged, we expended the last of our artillery. I crept forward on all fours during the silence and peered cautiously into the dining room. The last two intruders were dead, huddled in a mangled pile of punctured flesh and shattered bone.

Our victory was secured, and we joined the others upstairs. Caroline held John's head in her lap as she rocked back and forth, crying. Kevin had been applying pressure to the entry wound on his back, but it didn't help. The bullet must have been hollowed at the tip, as it had exploded his chest on exit. Wiping the blood from his hands on his t-shirt, Kevin said hollowly, "He's gone."

Seth, Connor, and I each lowered our heads in turn. Sidney was now leaning over the railing at the top of the stairs. Sonny, Fred, and Earl, who'd been out in the woods when the shooting commenced, burst through the front door, arriving too late to do anything. Luckily, Sara hadn't returned yet from the barn.

The fight was over. And then there were ten.

Chapter Twenty-Nine

John was dead now, shot through the back. Jesus, his blood was thick and dark. As we gathered in the front hall, where Kevin and Seth eventually laid out John's body, Caroline still holding his hand, a strange buzzing sound filled my head. The room spun slowly as I seemed to leave my body, floating overhead, watching each of my friends react.

Had Connor dug his latest hole for John? Maybe he wasn't predicting his own death at all. Maybe he knew on some unconscious level that we'd require another grave. We fill one, and he goes right to work preparing another. Who would be next?

Caroline was inconsolable. Sara returned and tried desperately to comfort her, but Caroline had difficulty buying the whole God concept. She was wrought with guilt, blaming herself for John's death. No one could argue the point, but to keep her from blowing her head off, we had to sell her on the idea that shit happens.

*****

A few nights later, I sat on the ledge outside my bedroom window, smoking a joint and trying to forget. This had become a nightly habit for me, but it wasn't working tonight, so I turned to climb back through the window.

Then my bedroom door opened. Shrinking back and out of view, I watched Connor enter the room, followed closely by Sara, who closed the door gently behind her so as not to make a sound. The two sat on *my bed* with their backs to me, unaware of my invasion on their conversation. What were they doing? I suddenly felt utterly betrayed.

I listened as they whispered back and forth. What the hell was going on? Since when were Connor and Sara close? Come to think of it, hadn't I seen them together a few times lately? But suddenly, they were secreting themselves away in my bedroom. For what purpose? Were they becoming involved? Were they planning on overthrowing me... my authority? A picture forms in my mind of Sara rolling her eyes at all the times I'd tried to act like a leader. I clutched at my chest as if to silence my quickening heart. The pounding became ridiculous, almost audible. Before I could listen to any more of their conversation, I slid away from the window, worried that my labored breathing might give me away.

I made my way to the antenna at the south corner of the house, where I could climb to the ground. The blood roared in my ears as I recalled the sight of Connor's arm reaching around Sara's shoulders, comforting her.

"Who goes there?" Someone called from the addition: Freddy, I think.

"It's me!" I shouted back at him. "It's Joel." I was sweating now and uncomfortable in my own skin.

"Sorry, Joel!" he responded. The echo of his voice rang in my ears as it took on Connor and Sara's voices, and I lost consciousness.

*****

I woke up in my bed hours later. Earl was seated on my couch, playing with Rex. No one else was in the room. Outside, it was dark.

"They're plotting against me," I whispered to him.

"Say again?"

"They're plotting against me." I struggled to sit up. "They were talking about me."

Returning my T-Rex to his place on my desk, Earl tried to make sense of what I'd said. "What? Who? When?"

"Just today, right here, in my room."

"Joel, who is plotting against you?" Earl was captivated.

"Forget it." I sank back onto the pillows.

He looked disappointed.

"I was just rambling."

"Okay, well, since you're up and better, I've got to head out to Skylab for my shift at the window. You gonna be okay? Sara checked you over and said you got a couple of nasty bruises but no broken bones."

I winced at her name. "Sure, go ahead."

"Yell if you need anything." With that, Earl left the room, closing the door behind him.

I replayed what I'd heard of the conversation between Sara and Connor repeatedly in my mind. Each time I closed my eyes, the dialogue would start again, my teeth grinding behind quivering lips.

"He's an *addict*, Connor," Sara exclaimed. "He's changing, changing into someone that honestly scares me."

I was an addict? *Really?*

"Sara, I know he's been dipping into the bag a lot more than the rest of us, but he's got the most riding on his shoulders."

Atta boy Connor, let her know. Make her understand. "I can't say I would react any differently," he admitted.

"Oh *bullshit*, Connor. We let Joel get away with it because of who he is. We turned a blind eye, me because I'm in this relationship with him, you and the rest because you respect him." Jesus, she wasn't pulling any punches. This was what the person who *loved me* thought of me.

"Alright, Sara, alright. You're right. I was aware of the problem and hoped it would work itself out, but you're right; he's slipping away. We're losing him to the drug."

Connor changed his tune pretty quickly. Why? He thought I was a junkie too? That's bullshit! He was looking to get on her good side, but why? What was his real objective? Did he miss Julia so much that he'd stab his best friend in the back to score with my girlfriend?

"I can't do it anymore, Connor. I can't let him fall into that life. And if he's intent on doing this, I can't be with him." She was crying now, crocodile tears. She can't love me. No one could say those things about someone they really loved. Connor wrapped his arm around her shoulders, and she leaned into him. What was happening here? What was he doing?

"I'll talk to him. I need to talk to him anyway."

"What will you say?" Silence. "No, I can't let you confront him; I have to tell him."

Tell me. Tell me what? That you think I've turned into some fucking junkie? That you prefer Connor over me? Fuck you! Fuck both of you!

"Fuck that!" I shouted, not giving a shit who might hear me.

Opening my eyes, I saw no one. Only Rex sat on the desk where Earl had left him.

"So what? Huh, Rex?" I addressed my conscience from across the room. "So, I'm a junkie now. So, I'm not good enough, so I'm human!" My throat tightened. "Why couldn't we have just died with the rest of them? Huh? Screw a second chance!" I swallowed hard.

Rex had little to offer as I ranted. Finally, I stopped myself. My eyes closed as I fell back onto my pillows. As hate replaced sadness and loathing devolved into hate, I realized I was hopelessly alone. Cupping my hands over my face, I cried. Or did I laugh? Like I'd said before, who could make the distinction anymore?

Lighting a bowl, I pulled the drug into my lungs, held my breath, and passed out.

*****

When I regained consciousness, Sara sat on the bed, gazing down at me. Noticing I was awake, she said, "I like you best like this."

"Like what?" I asked. "On my back?"

"Calm. At peace." Smiling sadly, she ran her fingers through my hair. "You're such a good man, and I do love you, Joel."

Tears. She was going to break the news to me, perhaps an ultimatum. I knew she wasn't going to stay with me.

"I think it's time for a change, Sara." I squeezed her hand harder than I meant to as I removed it from my head. "I've been thinking. With everything happening to me... until I've figured it all out, maybe we'd better sleep in separate rooms."

There, I'd said it. I took the hit. For some reason, I wanted to make it easy for her.

"Joel, I..."

"Just go," I said, cutting her off. "I'm not the same person I was, and I don't think he's coming back. I'm on a path I can't alter, and I think it's time to accept it. You'll have to do the same." I let go of her hand. She slowly released her grip on mine. After wiping her face, she got up and closed the door behind her.

Alone once again, I felt miserable. But I could not forget what I had seen and heard. They had disrespected my authority. They sought comfort in each other's arms, abandoning me! I got up, went to my desk, and packed a pipe to settle my nerves. After smoking the bowl, I crawled back into bed and covered myself with the tattered comforter. I wept. Then I slept. It was the only place I was really comfortable anymore.

Chapter Thirty

The following morning, I was in Skylab with Connor and Freddy for the 8:00 a.m. shift. We watched the sun creep over the horizon, igniting the sky. Then I asked Freddy to bring me some more ammunition. I needed him out of the room: before coming on shift, I'd hidden the bullet boxes for my sidearm, ensuring he would be searching awhile.

After he'd left, I faced Connor. "I sent him out on purpose. I want to talk to you."

"What's up?"

"Connor," I said slowly, deliberately. "Did you and Sara have a little talk about me yesterday?"

"Yesterday?" He stared at me. Damn it, he even looked confused.

"Yesterday," I reiterated. My face was solemn, and in a flash, so was his. He knew now that I had either heard everything or been tipped off somehow.

"Yes. We did." His eyes never left mine. "Nothing bad about you. Just some general concerns because we both care."

"Spending a lot of time together lately, aren't you?"

The questions were becoming accusations: I wasn't holding back.

"What?" That was all he could say. He'd been caught. There, I'd caught him now, now I knew. I felt dizzy.

"I told Sara last night that I wasn't going to be with her anymore, that she was a free woman." My adrenaline was surging.

For someone who was sleeping with my girlfriend, he seemed pretty upset. "That's the fucking stupidest thing that's ever come out of your mouth, man!"

"Hey, since I'm a junkie, maybe she belongs with someone better."

"Where are you getting all of this?! What the fuck is wrong with you?!" He shouted.

Wrong with me? Was he kidding?

"Don't yell at me, don't you fucking yell at me! This is *your* fault! You did this to *me!* You want her? She's yours!" I strode over to him. He did not flinch, although the anger and bewilderment never left his expression.

My anger spilled out as I yelled my accusations into his face.

He continued to deny it. Sara came running into the addition with Fred and Sonny. Seth and Sidney soon followed, attracted by the yelling. As I panned each of their faces, I saw shock and horror.

"Stop it! Stop it!!" Sara cried, rushing past Fred and Sonny to get between Connor and me. "Why are you fighting?"

She looked terrible. Her skin was white; dark circles marked her puffy, red-rimmed eyes. Behind her, the guys looked like they'd just been kicked in the bag. They'd never seen us at each other's throats like this before.

"This is between me and him. I don't want any of you here!" I shouted.

"It's okay, Sonny," Connor said. "Just go."

"Why are you fighting?!" Tears streaked her cheeks.

"It's nobody's business, Sara!" I snapped.

"We'll be done in a minute," Connor told Sonny, who refused to budge.

"You're a real piece of work, Connor!" I could hold back no longer. The blood roared in my ears. "I'll give 'em something to talk about!"

My fist slammed into his face, knocking him to the floor. I moved to boot him in the ribs, but the other guys intervened, ending the one-sided battle as quickly as it had begun.

Connor let Sonny and Fred help him to his feet and lead him out. He muttered something under his breath as he touched his jaw gingerly. To the others, he added, "Don't let him near the drugs."

Sid and Seth released me when Connor cleared the room. Sara asked them to leave us, and they did, albeit reluctantly.

"What's wrong with you?" she wept. "What would possess you? Your best friend?" She was sitting on the floor with her hands supporting her head. I stayed on the floor as well, shaking uncontrollably.

"I know all about you two. I heard your conversation yesterday." My tone was covered in a layer of frost so palpable the whole room seemed to cool. My heart was pounding violently, and my breathing became ragged as the adrenalin pushed through my veins.

"What the hell does that mean? What? What about us?" She had managed to look angry and innocent simultaneously, no easy feat.

"Don't do that, Sara. Don't treat me like an idiot. Give me that, at least."

"Joel, I..." Her voice broke. "Joel, these things are IN YOUR HEAD."

"You're saying I dreamed up that conversation? 'Cause if that's what you're suggesting, then you'd better rethink your next words, or this conversation is over."

"Stop it! Just stop it, alright?" She banged her palm on the plywood flooring. "We *did* have a conversation about you yesterday. But not to drag you through the mud. You've been giving us reason to worry about you. I'm allowed to *talk* to Connor, aren't I?"

"You've been talking a lot lately, Sara." I was losing what little composure I had left. "You two have been doing a lot of *talking* lately."

"Did you ever stop to think about *why* that could be?" she shouted. "Did you ever think that maybe if you didn't bury your emotions and thoughts in that goddamn pipe daily, two or three times a day, we could talk like we used to?"

"The drugs are keeping me together right now, alright?!" I yelled back. "They're *helping* me cope!"

"The drugs are *killing* you, Joel!"

"They keep me sane!"

"They're making you *insane!* The pot is making you paranoid! The more you use it, the worse you get! You don't see it, but *we* do!" She wiped her eyes. "It's making you crazy, Joel. And I don't want that for you. I don't."

"But you'll fuck Connor in the meantime, is that it?! *Is it?!* Well, fuck you and your bullshit half-assed concern because I'll be fine! I'm better off on my own."

I scrambled to my feet and left Sara on the floor, weeping. Storming blindly downstairs and out the door, I jumped onto one of the Harleys we'd collected. For a fleeting second, I felt like an asshole for leaving her in such a state of misery, but righteous indignation soon took over. I'd been deceived. I'd lost face with everyone, been humiliated, embarrassed, and betrayed! How could she do that to me? How could I face any of them again?

I had no idea where I was going. But I would soon find out. And it would mean the end of everything.

Chapter Thirty-One

Passing the abandoned north gate, which had been dismantled months before to tighten our defenses and shorten our supply lines, I resolved to keep going until something, or someone made me stop.

I was sure Connor and Sara, the two people whom I'd trusted the most, had betrayed me. Their deceit made me question everything.

I checked my pockets for a spare bag of bud. The bike swerved from left to right as my concentration shifted, but I steadied her. Good- I found a half-quarter. Pulling onto the shoulder, I parked the motorcycle and sat on the road divider. James Bong was tucked into another pocket, so I eagerly packed and lit the bowl.

I inhaled several times before exhaling, holding the smoke captive in my lungs and shaking my head to speed up the process. My heart was broken; my life was over. Yet, strangely, it made me love Sara more, *want* to love her more and show her how much I appreciated her. But the thought of her and Connor... *Bitch!*

Bang! I was hit. My mouth fell open, my eyes closed, and my head pitched back. The painful thoughts were still there but distant now. I could focus only on what was happening in the here and now. I waited until I felt steadier, then mounted the bike and resumed my journey.

Continuing north, I passed where we'd seen the farmer's cattle stampede across the road while the forest beyond his home burned. That was when things were in their infancy and could've gone either way. As I rode by, I saw the grey, collapsed farmhouse, suffering the full extent of my neighbor's misfortune. Or was it their good fortune? Nothing good had come of us making it this far.

Turning right, I headed east with no purpose in mind but to keep moving. Thoughts came and went with little effort or accompanying emotion. The smile remained on my face; the bike motored on.

Sure, the wind in my face was artificial, but it was freeing. After feeling like I'd been on a path I had no control over, I was finally making my way, pushing through. Then, I became reflective: As humans, we were constantly *pushing*. We pushed the limits of everything. We pushed our environment. We pushed each other. We were a race of bullies. On the flip side, we pushed through adversity. We pushed through hardships and impossible scenarios. We didn't necessarily come out on top, but we did try, didn't we?

Green signs whizzed past me, announcing town names and their former population totals. I recalled that Elle Lake would soon appear to my left. As I took the bend, the bike seemed to know where it was going. Besides, could I detour from my destiny? Whatever I did, destiny would find me.

Squeezing my eyes shut, I tested my theory. The sensation was incredible. It was as though I were invincible. Then, ten seconds later, I veered off and crashed through the dead saplings and thick, dead brush that lined the ditch. Caught in the face by a low-hanging branch, I was thrown from my seat and landed solidly on my tailbone while the bike slammed into a stump and flipped over.

Slumped there, watching the bike's front wheel spin, I felt dizzy and collapsed onto the dusty earth. Looking up, I saw the blackened trees above me reaching ever upwards toward the sun, longing for a second chance. I closed my eyes and blacked out.

*****

When I regained consciousness, I still lay on my back, arms at my sides. Slowly, carefully, I sat up. I could hear something.

It was unmistakable. I could hear people in the woods below. People! I found my pistol, lowered myself onto my stomach, and aimed toward their voices. Then, suddenly, they stopped. I listened carefully but heard nothing further.

Had they only been in my head? Strange, they had seemed real enough. I waited what seemed like an eternity before letting my guard down. Then I rose, picked up my bike, and pushed through the sloping hill's brush. Suddenly, a small encampment appeared so suddenly in front of me that I froze. Was it real?

A voice rang out. A dreadfully familiar voice. "Joel!"

Gareth.

My fingers gripped the motorcycle handlebars so tightly that my knuckles cracked in protest. My pistol was holstered inside my coat, but I'd have been cut down before I could go for it.

Several flag people materialized from the woods around me, closing in. Gareth was approaching from the direction of the camp, his smile cruel.

"Wait!" I said. His pace slowed, and I thought fast.

"I- I've come here to see you." The words were out of my mouth before I could process what I was saying.

Gareth lit up. He looked at his followers as if to say, I told you so. Then he approached, his manner more relaxed.

"Knew you would," he said, almost gleefully. "Knew you would..." Smiling through that filthy beard, he reached me and slapped my shoulders in a manner not unfriendly. I remained glued to the bike, afraid that any movement on my part might spark a violent reaction from the others.

"Give our guest some room, people!" Gareth shouted, noticing my discomfort. The group fell away. I dropped the bike and let him lead me toward the camp.

"Just give me their name, Joel," he said. "The one you are here to present to us. Did you bring them?"

"Their name?" I repeated, trying not to sound confused. Any indecision would turn the situation violent; I felt it.

"Yes, Joel. A sympathizer: You found one in your midst. I can tell. A traitor to your cause." He began shaking his head again. "I was tipped off by a divine vision that you would visit and present us with this gift."

The group studied me. Nothing can describe the extreme angst I experienced standing there. Thought escaped me; my head went empty. Please, I did not want this to be my destiny. After all I'd been through, I wasn't going to find my end at the hands of Gareth and his religious rejects.

"Tell me then, tell us, who has wronged you?" Gareth breathed through his mouth, wheezing, the wiry hairs surrounding his lips pushing out with each exhalation. The group seemed to sway back and forth as they waited patiently for my answer.

Two people had wronged me, but only one name came to mind. I *hated* him; I was sure I hated him. I couldn't let it end here. I wasn't ready to die, not like this. So, I spoke the name.

Gareth smiled like a jackal.

My heart sank, and I cringed. What had I done? What did it matter? I had offered Gareth a lamb and saved my own neck. My mind began to race. I was offering a friend to certain death. But if he were out of the picture, it would solve many more problems for me than it would create! I could never hurt him like that myself... No, my part had to be such that no one could suspect me. I couldn't let the others know this was my doing.

"It is done." Gareth savored this phrase as he would a good meal. "It is done!" This time, he shouted, raising his arms triumphantly to the excited crowd around us.

They began to mass-chant the name of my former friend, my treacherous, conniving, back-stabbing *friend*. I looked slowly around the circle, knees shaking, while they praised me as the latest inspiration driving the flag army toward a new hope. Bile rose in my throat. I pushed through the tightly packed circle, staggered into a bush, and vomited.

Gareth followed me. When I stopped heaving, he laid a reassuring hand on my back. "Joel, we have you to thank for our renewed strength."

"Then you let me do this my way," I replied, breathing through my nose until the nausea subsided. "I'll set this up for you, but I don't want any credit for your continued success; you understand me, Gareth?"

One more brutal convulsion followed my demand, painful and deliberate. The muscles in my back ached, and my throat burned.

"There will be no mention of you, Joel," he promised. "No one will know you had any part in this. Come, you will spend the night with us. We will discuss a plan of action over dinner." He spoke as if he'd intended to discuss plans for a surprise party.

After drinking some water from a surprisingly clean cup, I took out my pipe and lit up without asking permission, needing to escape into oblivion. Gareth said nothing, just watching me with unholy glee warming his features. Something stood behind him, something dark. Was it a shadow? No, it left me cold. Escaping worked. I remained there on my knees for some time.

*****

Later that evening, I sat with Gareth and his followers before a fire that roasted a small animal carcass. The smell was all-encompassing, triggering a powerful memory.

It was a memory from camping, one of many I will now have to forget: meat cooking over an open flame, my friends surrounding me, my Sara next to me. A single tear tracked the contours of my cheek, and I brushed it away angrily. It was my destiny to carry out this plan of Gareth's. Sara and Connor were dead to me, and I was alone. I wouldn't be discouraged. The word destiny repeated itself over and over in my head, lulling me into a trance. It was all I had left to believe in.

Gareth watched as I tilted my head back, closed my eyes, and breathed deeply, enjoying the heady cooking scent permeating the air.

"They're all over these parts," he told me, gesturing toward the carcass, which had been removed from the flame and laid on a platter. Snapping away a few meaty ribs, he handed them to me. I didn't need to be asked twice: shit, I hadn't eaten a piece of fresh meat in months. Biting down on the charbroiled flesh was rejuvenating. I felt like a person again. Like a man.

"Good, yes?" Gareth looked amused as he watched me tear into the meat so eagerly grease covered my lips and chin.

"It's good," I confirmed.

"We don't waste a single organ: even the tongue and eyes are eaten. It is the perfect balance. We use everything we catch. We use the animal completely."

When the meal was over and some members began cleaning up, Gareth took me aside so that the real business could be tabled. The first thing he wanted to know was what my friend looked like.

"I'll point him out to you," I replied.

"How can we be sure the others will not retaliate? Could you take him to a secluded spot?"

I shook my head. "I wasn't exactly on good terms with anyone when I left. If I took him away with me and returned without him, they'd suspect I'd had a part in it. No, they'll have to witness his death."

"They'll have to be unarmed."

"That's not going to happen. They're too used to carrying guns everywhere."

"Then we're at an impasse, and that is unfortunate." Irritation hardened his tone. "I won't march into your stronghold without a guarantee that my people will come to no harm. I offer you the same."

"I'll make it happen. I have to figure out how I'll get everyone outside. I'll need more than your word: you'll only take *him* and hurt no one else." I meant it. I was determined to see my destiny through to completion but had to insist no one else be harmed.

"You have my word, Joel. That is all I can give." He rose. "We leave in the morning."

After bidding me goodnight, he disappeared into his trailer. I walked back to my bike. Leaning against the motorcycle and methodically licking and sucking the dried fat from my fingers, I told myself: I could kill them all right now. *I could.* I could take my spare gasoline canister, pour it all over their camp, and throw it into the fire.

But I couldn't, much as I wanted to. I needed them now. I needed them to complete my destiny.

Strangely, I slept soundly.

Chapter Thirty-Two

The ride back to the house was like a bad dream. It was happening. It was *really* happening.

After camp was broken and the RVs rolled out, I started my bike and assumed the lead position. Gareth raised a hand to me as I passed, his eyes fixated on the road ahead. I had to hand it to the son of a bitch- he was driven. Even during that fateful moment when we'd reclaimed our freedom, he had not for an instant played the victim. Maybe he could sense a destiny playing out; maybe he'd always known. Maybe that was why he never lost his edge. He could accept his destiny, where I had failed to do so.

Pulling ahead of the pack by half a mile gave me enough time to stop a moment and light the pipe. Shaking my head violently, I looked back to see whether the caravan had caught up. When they drew close, I pulled back onto the road, tires spitting the loose gravel behind me.

I stopped and dismounted when we were roughly two miles from the house. Gareth got out of his RV and approached.

"This is as far as I want your trucks," I told him. "The rest of the distance we'll cover on foot."

Gareth agreed, turned to his followers, and signaled them to exit the vehicles.

"When we arrive, I want you to sit tight in the back woods until you see me appear by the pool." I scratched my face and rubbed the end of my nose. I had trouble hiding that I was anything but straight, but I did my damnedest. "When I'm at the pool, I'll have everyone out front and ready in about five minutes."

"Understood." He turned to address his group. "Everyone hear that? When Joel reveals himself, we will slowly move in, flanking either side of the house, closing in on his position at the front." Turning back to me, he added, "Will we be certain not to run into any resistance?"

"If I had wanted you dead, you would be," I said, assuring him that my friends would not fire unless fired upon. "They are trained to follow my orders. If I order their guns down, then they'll do it."

"Be sure that you do. I'm not looking for a bloodbath: I want the sympathizer."

With those chilling words, we began our approach. After positioning the flags safely beyond our defenses, I left Gareth with a final order. "Do not fuck this up. You have one chance at this. We can't afford any screw-ups."

He nodded.

The walk back to the house took me past the graves of Jake, Julia, and Gil. Beside their sites was an ominous, yawning hole, the latest fruit of Connor's dark obsession. I stopped and knelt at its edge.

What a thing, I thought. What a thing to do, Connor, what a burden to carry. "You've gone and dug your own hole." I rose and kicked loose dirt into the abyss. "You knew the whole time, didn't you? You *knew*. You fuckin' knew. So why didn't you do something to stop it? Why did you let it go this far?"

An indifferent silence offered no reply. I turned away and continued toward the house.

Sonny, who was on duty in Skylab, saw me approach. He alerted the others, who met me in the kitchen as I entered through the second floor sliding doors.

"Joel!" Sara cried. She rushed toward me, but the scowl on my face stopped her cold. "Where have you been?"

"Clearing my head." I avoided eye contact. "I'm back now, though." A pause. I had to do this. "Where's Connor? I need to see him."

Sara looked pleased at the question. "He's been pretty eager to see you too, Joel."

"So, *where* is he?" I asked again.

"He's in his room," Seth spoke up. "Good to see you. We were getting worried."

"Thanks." I went up the stairs, heart pounding. I wanted to confront him, see him, and accept that I was fulfilling a destiny bigger than both of us. Reaching his door, I hesitated a moment. Across the hall, I could see Rex lying on my bed, looking at me.

"What!?" I whispered to him. "Shut up!" This was not the time for him to start talking. Then, quickly, abruptly, I knocked on Connor's door.

"Come in." Connor sounded despondent.

I opened the door. He was sitting cross-legged on his bed, elbows resting on his knees and eyes on the floor. When he looked up and saw me, his eyes didn't brighten. "Hey," he said.

"Hey." I forced myself to smile. "I've got to ask you to come out front with me, you and the others. It's important."

"I had a déjà-vu last night," he started.

Shit!

"It involves you, Joel. And me."

"I don't want to hear it," I told him, shaking my head and blinking madly.

"Well, you're going to." His tone was lifeless. "So, you'll want to sit, old man, and listen to my dying declaration."

My whole body went numb. He knew. I sank into an old rocking chair.

"Your paranoid delusions are delusions. But they're also your reality. The déjà-vu has shown me everything. What has happened, what is about to happen, and what will happen when we're both gone. I saw it all." He stopped. "We're players, Joel, and destiny will be realized no matter our choices. Though the choices we make are our own, destiny is not something that can be so easily derailed."

Tears collected in my eyes. I willed them back.

"I know what you think you saw is as real as this conversation. I get that." He paused. "So now it's up to you. Do you listen to the voices in your head?"

"Aren't I supposed to?" I interrupted.

"Or do you look to common sense?" He continued, unfazed. "I can't judge you either way. I have to trust you'll make the right decision… for you."

"I…" I couldn't speak.

"So, let's go outside."

We stepped slowly into the hallway, Connor leading the way with purpose in his every step. This was it. I could stop it. But he wouldn't let me. He felt the march of destiny forcing each forward step as I did. I moved through the scene as if being carried forward by a current stronger than myself. I couldn't stop now. The fear was overwhelming. Fear for Connor. Fear for the life to follow, but also a fear of not following through. Upon descending the staircase, I saw that the bulk of our clan had come to meet us in the front hall.

As I approached the back of the house, I heard Connor explain that we would be meeting on the front lawn. I stopped in front of the back door and held the handle for several moments. The metal felt cold in my hand. My muscles twitched. Turn the knob. Do it. Turn the knob. My stomach churned. I willed myself to remember my hurt and hatred towards my friend. I let it linger on an image of Connor and Sara together on my bed. I was ridding myself of an enemy now. I couldn't trust him. I made myself feel sure I could never trust him again. I turned the knob.

I went to the pool, knowing I was visible to Gareth's troops. In five minutes, Connor would be at their mercy. There was now no way for me to stop this. I had made my choice.

I passed the group in the front hall, and everyone followed me outside. I approached them, each eying me expectantly. I stood next to Connor, ensuring that Gareth's people would not take out the wrong 'sympathizer,' and studied the surrounding trees, knowing that the flags would emerge when I gave the sign. My friends' guns were either holstered or slung over their shoulders, unprepared for the act that would momentarily play out before them. I opened my mouth to talk and was interrupted by the rush of footfalls.

We were surrounded almost immediately after I'd laid a hand on Connor's shoulder. My friends froze, unable to comprehend what was happening. I envied their ignorance. The flags relieved them of their firearms. Then they grabbed Connor by the arms, pulling him aside. Enraged, Sonny slammed a powerful fist into the face of one of Connor's captors. The man dropped to his knees, groaning and bleeding. His comrades aimed their weapons at Sonny's head.

"Stop!" Connor cried. "Don't react, Sonny. Please. I don't want anyone to die here."

"You would be wise to listen to him, *Sonny*." Gareth appeared next to Connor, staring at him as he addressed us. "Connor knows what he's done. A secret supporter of the Reaper's ideals."

Gareth now faced the group. My friends regarded him with fear and hatred. We were corralled against the garage doors.

"Connor is a classic sympathizer. He cannot be changed, only destroyed!" He relished his moment.

Sara whimpered. Her feelings were betraying her: proof that she favored Connor now. Caroline was shaking and crying. Sidney comforted her. Earl's eyes met mine as he realized what was about to happen; I could tell he was trying desperately to keep from charging the nearest flag member. I shook my head, and he relaxed, acknowledging we would not stand a chance.

Forcing Connor to his knees, Gareth waved in his depleted forces, keeping a hard line on our movements. Connor was looking at me. Tears fell to the dusty earth as his head bent forward. Helpless to change what had come to pass, I couldn't feel anything anymore. In that split second, the exact second it took for Gareth to end my friend's life, I did not exist.

Then suddenly, as if the gunshot blast had awoken all my senses, the paranoia, hate, and jealousy left me. There was Connor, face in the dirt, blood trickling from a hole in the back of his head, silent, dead. I could no longer stand. I lost the use of my legs and sank onto the ruinous earth beneath me, just as Connor had. I was not the first to fall; I was not the last. We were all experiencing the same nightmare.

Chapter Thirty-Three

Their bloody deed accomplished, the army left, as promised, weapons trained on us as they returned to their vehicles.

Caroline screamed after them. "Murdering bastards!"

"I'll get you! Every fucking one of you!" Sonny yelled through his shock.

I let them vent their pain and rage as I crawled to Connor. He was warm. I gathered him in my arms and cradled him against my chest. The exit wound on his forehead oozed blood over his blackened eyes and bruised face. I closed his eyes and rocked back and forth, letting the blood cover my chest and stain me with my guilt. Connor was dead. What had I done?

My friends gathered around, watching silently as I struggled with my grief. Unable and unwilling to release him, staggered by the magnitude of the act, I focused on how I had brought it about. Throwing my head back, I cried out. The sound of my anguish sent some reeling backward, my pain echoing off the house. It was a sound that would reverberate in my head for the rest of my life.

The others left me alone with Connor, understanding only that I had lost my best friend. I remained on the front lawn for hours, cradling him. I kept talking to him like old times, and this nightmare had been erased. I stayed with him until the body was cold and ridged, and the others, unaware of my role in this catastrophe, urged me to come inside.

I picked Connor up; his stiffening limbs made it difficult as I positioned him across my shoulders. I wanted him buried, comfortable, and to do it myself as a last favor to him. But when I took my first step toward the graveyard, my legs gave out, and I collapsed. Slowly, I rolled his heavy frame off of me as the others hurried over to assist.

Sonny, Earl, Kevin, and I carried Connor to the site. The rest followed. Sara didn't pray this time but looked on in stony silence. I helped lay him into the grave he had made for himself and covered him with the soil as carefully as I might have tucked a child into bed.

The ceremony over, I walked slowly from the graveyard into the woods, hoping that I could also leave behind the feelings of guilt and betrayal, buried forever with Connor in the fetid earth. The group gave me the space that I needed and returned to the house in a solemn, devastated procession.

Passing the shed and its attendant memories, I continued to the outer perimeter of our property and crawled over the rusted fencing. The daylight was fading, but the sky above remained undaunted by the scattered clouds to the north. Finding a spot next to a dry riverbed, I sat and picked at the dead foliage around me.

In the silence of the woods, I recalled the biblical story of Judas and the betrayal. Stunned, I realized we were one and the same. The revulsion I felt for that traitor, in reading the biblical story of betrayal, I now felt for myself. "What made you do it, Judas?" I wondered. "Was it the silver? I doubt it. Was it your destiny? Did a little angel make you do it?"

I laughed, nausea billowing in my stomach as I poked at the dry earth with a lifeless twig. The burden I now bore, which had overwhelmed me at Connor's death, surged in me again. I'd done a terrible thing. If someone or something had told me to do this, it wasn't God or a guardian angel. It was my ego poisoning me all along. I had listened, and this is where it had gotten me. Bobbing back and forth on my haunches, I could not control the deep regret. The feeling was so overpowering that my vision blurred, and my strength left me. I crashed onto my back, hands covering my face.

My pain echoed around me as the ruined forest became my Father Confessor. The world seemed cold as my suffering intensified with each passing moment. Opening my eyes to the cruel environment, I quieted the sounds of an unequaled pain radiating from deep within me. The few wavering clouds that had drifted in from the north had now accumulated overhead, growing in size, reaching from one end of my peripheral to the other.

My side ached, so I jabbed one hand under my ribs to ease the cramp. Breathing deeply to soften the pain, I watched the clouds overtake the sun. A foreboding shadow now labored its way across the forest, shielding me from the judgment I felt weighing me down. What was taking place here? What was developing up there? Then, suddenly, a drop fell from the sky. A drop! It hit my face, followed by others.

"Rain..." It was almost too much for me to bear. "Rain."

Connor would never see this now. Connor would have seen this had he still been alive. I wept for things that would never be, things that could never be. The rain came in force now, beating down on the tortured soil. Running back toward the shack, I stumbled over the fencing. Picking myself up, I reached the building and pushed through the door, landing hard on the ground.

The rain stung, but was it only because it was falling so hard, so suddenly, or was the acid rain coming back to finish us off? My mind raced. I poked my head out the door of my childhood clubhouse, hand cautiously extended. It did not burn. I cupped my hands and drank. It was good.

"Rain," I repeated aloud. A smile broke the frown. Things would be better now; things would grow...

Wham! Pain exploded on my forehead. I had hit myself, eliminating the warm glow I had felt for that split second. I was in no position to savor this rain or what hope it might offer. I had no right!

"Fuck!" I shouted.

Wham! Again, I hit myself, my nose spraying blood from the right nostril. Who was this hitting me? Who *was I*? I couldn't allow myself another moment's pleasure, and if I was to become some masochist, so be it. I kept hitting myself, each blow harder than the last, picking out new spots on my face that hadn't yet felt the sting of my shame.

Once satisfied that I had sufficiently stopped the good feelings, I sat on the dirty armchair, a flurry of dust exploding from its worn cushions. Blood drooled from the corner of my mouth. My teeth had cut the inside of my cheek. I rubbed my jaw and nose, concentrating on the pain. The rain continued to hammer down on the metal roof.

I couldn't go on like this. Judas had played out the destiny promised him. I, too, would have to complete the course I was fated to follow.

*****

I entered the house through the kitchen door. A heavy silence dominated throughout. My friends sat on the balcony overlooking the backyard, watching my approach, watching the rain. Without a word to them, I went upstairs to my room.

Sidney called to me from the front hall.

"Joel! The rain… It's good…."

I didn't answer him. I couldn't, as the lump had returned to my throat. I rounded the banister and made my way up to my room. The thought of what I had to do to make things right weighed heavily on my mind, stirring up several new emotions. In my room, where I made my final preparations, smoking the pipe was a matter of extreme urgency.

What a joke I was, what a victim! How could I ever look at myself in the mirror again? I couldn't live with myself. My path was clear - I would end my existence myself if the gods couldn't see their way clear to do it for me. Fuck the angel and his grand plan, fuck 'em! The circle broke here; no more, Joel, no more pandering!

Epilogue

Only now, in my most crucial hour, do I feel that I should let my friends know what had transpired to bring me to this end.

With paper and pen in hand, I sit at my desk. It's roughly seven forty-five in the evening. My pen moves across the paper, composing the letter explaining everything. Tears resurface at the realization of how dramatically I've changed, how far a cry I am from the Joel who existed before the Reaper struck.

But maybe if someone comes in, sees what I'm doing, and stops me, then maybe I won't do it. No. No, I have to do this. I can't live with what I've done. I don't deserve to!

Someone knocks softly on my door.

"Go away!" I answer, rising to my feet and falling heavily onto my couch. After a moment's pause, I hear footsteps receding.

I slowly knock the back of my head against the couch's wooden frame. The repetition is therapeutic. With each blow, I cement the idea of taking my own life. "There is nothing left of this one. Finish him." I hear or say; either way, I agree.

"Not yet!" I cry. "Not yet!" I must sound like a madman to the people I can now hear gathering outside my door. Picking up my fallen chair, I return to my desk and resume writing.

I can hear concerned murmuring out in the hall. I don't care. I can't look after these people anymore. My job was only to survive, never to lead.

That was their idea. I was never meant to be a leader. It had gone to my head. I had led them into misery and death. What did they have to hope for besides the rain? Had *I* brought the rain? Had Connor served as a sacrifice to some dated *god* who needed a blood offering to produce the rain?

I drop my pen and walk to my window. Sliding it open, I squeezed out of my room and lowered myself down the antenna to the wet ground. Stealing into the trees, I escape the scouting eyes in Skylab.

Without a course plotted, moving only to evade the conversation outside my door, I fall over an exposed root that the rains have washed free of its earthen prison and land hard in the muck. My face pressed against the slippery forest floor; I began to scratch the ground. Digging my fingers deep into the earth, I shovel out a great deal of the dirt, piling it next to me. My speed accelerates as the wet soil on my skin sends a rush through my body. Sitting upright, I summon my strength to pull up more dirt faster. The rainfall creates a small stream that tracks down the hill, washing over my efforts.

A small puddle of water collects in the hole I've made, softening the harder dirt so that I may continue my work. Looking to my right in the darkness, I see Jake's gravesite a few yards away, then Gil's, Julia's, and Connor's. Mine is not as deep as the others- not yet, but soon. I redouble my efforts, tackling rocks and roots, cutting my hands, and pulling back two fingernails. I ignore the pain.

Finally, the job is finished. My heart pounds while my fingers bleed. Looking to the sky, I let the rain fall on my face, cleaning the filth from my hands and arms.

"I'm going now!" I yell to the heavens as if they cared. I'd carried out their little plan. "Are you there!?" Where's my divine intervention now? My face is flushed, and my eyes burn. I feel like my head is going to explode. Don't fight it. Let it go.

Bowing my head, I surrender and resign myself to the knife. Standing and walking back toward the house, I feel strangely calm. My heart rate slows dramatically, and my breathing levels out while a feeling of acceptance overtakes me. This is my destiny to do this thing. Like Judas before me, I will carry out a similar end. Brilliant! Purpose!

The trip up the antenna seems speedy, the walk across the overhang effortless. Climbing through the window into my room, I accidentally step on Rex, crushing him. I offer an apology. He accepts it.

Searching my shelves, I find the Bowie knife I'd purchased some years ago and a partially full bottle of painkillers Sara gave me for the leg injury.

What else, though? What else would I need? Water, a bath perhaps, yes... something to bleed into, not like Julia, not all over the bed.

After carrying everything to the bathroom, I place the knife and pills on the counter and peer up at the Mickey Mouse clock above the toilet. It reads eight-thirty. A strange feeling overcomes me as I lock the bathroom door behind me. It is as though I've been here before, like a déja-vu. The thought sickens me. My stomach muscles contract violently, forcing up bile and burning my throat. I swallow it down.

"You're not me!" I speak to the mirror now. Spit hangs from my lips as I salivate rabidly. I am so far gone, so far removed - I can see that now. Shaking, I grip the granite countertop. "Stop staring at me!" I shout, throwing my fist into the reflection. Funny, I don't even cut myself.

When the mirror shatters, I snap out of my trance and pick up the pieces from the counter and floor. My sanity has left me. I sweep the mess into the garbage pail and pick up a spray cleaner and rag from a basket next to the toilet. In the periphery, I hear a knocking on the bathroom door and ignore it.

During the time it takes me to clean the bathroom, I recall a moment of my childhood: in the tub, with my mother watching, smiling, long before the unimagined pain. But of course, memories of my mother are all I've had these past seven months, and I had made peace with the fact that she and I would never share another moment, as my friends beyond the door would never share another with me. It is over. Once again, I feel at peace with the decision, accepting again what I must do, knowing that it is all I have left.

By ten-thirty, my work in the bathroom is through. I direct my attention to the cold porcelain tub and kneel beside it. When I suddenly shiver, a final thought enters my mind: who just walked over my grave?

The moment gone, I turn the cool water on, staggering my time.

"Death brings an honest response."

I hear it. Is it the angel? Turning slowly, I expect to see him standing at the door, prepared to talk me out of my decision.

"Death brings an honest response."

There it is again! No angel, though. Raising my hands to my ears, I momentarily block all external noise, the blood rushing through my head now amplified.

Pouring a glass of water from the sink, I shovel the painkillers into my mouth. Halfway there! I take the knife from the counter and spend a moment with it. Getting undressed, I step into the tub. The water is cold, but I immerse myself, dunking my head below its surface. I come up for a breath, pulling my hair back. My lips quiver as I think of the people I am leaving behind.

I feel alone, frightened, guilty. I sit in the tub long after I've gotten in, thinking, pondering, exploring. Looking at the clock, I see the time is five minutes to twelve. My lips stop quivering as I bite down on them.

The rain has ceased for now, but I know that as sure as the sun will shine tomorrow, the rain will follow, and life will be restored. Life will return for those who deserve it and can muster the strength to carry on.

I look at my wrist and then at the knife in my other hand. The knife is so sharp that my flesh will offer no resistance to one quick slash. That's all that it'll take, I tell myself. One quick motion, just one cut: then, release.

Pressing the blade against my wrist's softest and most tender area is easy. The steel is as cold as the water, and I feel nothing as I immerse my arm. They say it is painless. I wait for some signal that I may commence with the execution. Of course, there is no gun to sound or flag to fall. I am waiting only for myself to be ready to truly end the life that has plagued me so much in such a short time. It should be easier than this, I shouldn't hesitate...

Then it happens. I pull the blade down my forearm, tearing my flesh indiscriminately. It is not painless. My hand goes numb, but the gash throbs horribly. I drop the knife and breathe deeply. I watch my lifeblood color the water lightly at first and then darker with each passing second.

"My God..." I catch myself muttering. "My God..."

The scent of blood seeps out of the water, stinging my nose as I squirm uncontrollably. My first thought is of Sara, to yell out to her, but I stifle any attempt by covering my mouth with my one good hand. When calm, I lift my right arm out of the water. I can't help it. Curiosity has gotten the better of me.

The sight is overwhelming. My whole forearm is gashed so deeply that I can see tendons. I watch as blood spurts aimlessly from my wrist. I grasp at the wound, covering it. The feeling of blood escaping through my fingers is grotesque.

I've done it. There's no turning back now. Even if I wanted to, I'd be too faint to drag my near corpse out of the tub. I feel the color drain from my face. I am thirsty but fight the urge to dip my tongue into the ever-reddening water. Was I crazy to end it like this?

As I lie here in a shallow, watery grave, cold as death, I feel something through the dense haze of pills, something approaching euphoria. My death is an exit from a tormented existence. What I've done here is a mercy killing.

All that matters now is that I know peace. My head fills up with the idea of it. I giggle, this time losing all control. It comes in force now without reason or purpose. Perhaps the purpose is all too clear. It's funny that I should leave this world in such a state of peace, of joy. It's a beautiful feeling; the regret is forgotten. Joy, I have been denied too long.

And so, my life, such as it was, flows through my muddled head, on the edge of reality, much like my pending death. Like a high I can't come down from; I wouldn't want to. The giggling stops as abruptly as it began. My head slips under the cold sheet of red water. My sight blurs and sound is now reduced to a faint, sparse heartbeat underwater. It's so unreal.

The world is fluid. There is a knocking underwater and a tiny voice that accompanies it, calling my name. *Joel*. A murky image. Am I being lifted?

The last feeling I remember took me by surprise: it was the feeling of wrapping my arms around a tree. It was a little like love.

REBIRTH – BOOK TWO of The Judas Syndrome Trilogy

Sara Speaks....

I can't find my son. Anxiety overwhelms me. My heart pounds as I rush through the compound; in my panic, it seems more like a maze than the place I've called home for the past eight years. *Where is my son?*

The night comes alive as searchlights expose the darkness between buildings, igniting the tight spaces where a boy of eight might find himself. A sinister thought enters my head: *My mortal enemy currently shares this space with u*s. A renewed sense of urgency overcomes me, and my pace quickens.

*****

Your Father would have so loved you. You were a blessing when you were born, a mystery when you were conceived, and a terrible struggle while I carried you seven months in my belly. Seven months: It's not really long enough, but you seemed to time your arrival eerily close to the date of another's departure.

This place is like a concentration camp you'd see on TV when there was TV. Something from a Second World War movie. Did we live through the Third World War? Hard to say. Color is absent here: the walls are a battleship grey, the floors a polished concrete. It's not ideal surroundings for a baby to grow up in, but at least you grew up.

When we arrived, you were very small and still at my breast.

Somehow, we escaped a plague ravaging much of the surviving world.

Children are very important; so many died from this plague that took the young and very old. Most adults over sixty years old and those under twelve died soon after the Apocalypse, choked to death by fall-out, while those who survived were left to suffer this final indignity some months later. A plague, a flu of some design. I have worked closely with the doctors here, and they have not been able to succinctly label the disease that had methodically killed off so many.

The base was designed to train Special Forces in the war against terror. It has only a skeleton crew assigned to it, though it was expecting an influx of 1000 soldiers and their families the month following the end of life as we knew it. The base is well protected, with steel walls reaching 20 feet in places, outfitted with watch towers, a stockade, family housing, a mess hall, a hospital, and the central training and parade grounds. It even has a greenhouse.

The parade grounds are framed with civilian vehicles, RVs, camper vans, cars, and trucks of all shapes and sizes. They belong to those who fled the devastation to the south and came north. I recall the many motorcades we witnessed traveling north, right past Joel's house, where we had hidden out. We were fourteen friends, caught in something as unfathomable as the end of the world. Teenagers whose families had all been wiped out by one violent act against humanity. I remember talking to people as they stopped at the house. They said they were going on a *feeling*, going north.

The Sergeant told me that barely a year after most civilians had arrived, the plague had hit the base, and hundreds were quarantined. Almost all of them died, eventually. The base lost many of its own to the mysterious plague as well. The army doctors worked day and night to suppress the disease, to stop it in its tracks. In doing so, the hospital lost over 75% of its staff.

Finally, the plague had run its course. No more were dying or feeling feverish or showing red spots on their necks and torsos. Those who had survived, roughly half including the base personnel and civilians, would carry on, burn their dead, and start again.

*****

I remember asking about the water planes my friends, and I had seen putting out forest fires as we drove back to town, returning from our camping trip the day after the Reaper had followed through on his promise.

"They flew out of Kingston Air Force base," explained the captain. She removed her hat as she spoke. Her short blonde hair fell around her high cheekbones. She was an attractive woman, but she'd suffered an unimaginable loss, and the lines on her face mapped that story. "It's two days' drive west of us. They were retrofitted to do that job, those planes.

They would load up on water at Elle Lake and run water dumps all over the area. You said you were a good two-hour drive south of here, Sara?"

"Yes, about that," I replied.

"I'd say the planes would have penetrated just south of that and then west." She confirmed.

"We saw three or four at a time."

"Yes, you would have. They employed thirty-odd. They ran day and night for about 48 hours following the attack, and then, nothing."

"Nothing?" My voice cracked.

"We lost contact with them." The captain's tone was thoughtful.

"What happened to them?" I asked.

"Fatigue. The pilots wanted to keep flying. Keep up the momentum. Best we could tell, two of the bigger planes slammed into each other and the control tower while attempting to land and fuel up. They wiped out everyone, and with them, any chance for the other pilots to continue their work."

"That's so awful."

"We sent a patrol to investigate, and this was their conclusion." Her eyes met mine.

"No wonder you never came for us." My friends and I had hoped for a rescue for weeks after the sighting, believing that they had seen us and would come for us. But they never did.

"Even if we were made aware of your existence, it's unlikely we would have come for you. We were understaffed ourselves and had been ordered to stay put."

"Makes sense, I guess." But I wondered what my life would have been like had they come for us. Would Joel still be with me? Perhaps we would have succumbed like the others to the plague like the captain's husband and daughters had.

*****

The world wasn't always like this; perhaps it will be better one day. The military houses us now. They have graciously put us up here in the hope that you will survive, have your own children, and rebuild. That may sound like a lot to put on a child not yet eight years old but know that you are very special, and not just in the way only a mother can know.

Michael E. Poeltl

You would have had it so good in *life*. That's what we called it *before* the Reaper dropped the bombs: *life*. We were all someone else, kids barely out of high school. As the media had coined him, the Grim Reaper was a madman. A man, an organization, a country, no one really knew. The threat seemed almost laughable. But he wasn't laughing. He had demands that were never met; he had crazy ideals that required religions and governments to disappear. The things he asked were impossibilities. So, he showed us just how serious he was. The initial blasts killed our families. My friends and I had been spared, having taken a camping trip that weekend, *the weekend*. And when we returned, our worlds were changed forever. We, fourteen of us at first and within seven months only eight, managed to stay alive at my boyfriend's house in the country. We felt privileged, chosen to survive, to rebuild.

More than nine years ago, my life was very different. Was I lucky to have experienced life in all its normalcy and abundance? I think so; I still have my memories. Though sometimes my memories seem like little more than movies, something from someone's imagination.

The people here, the soldiers, believe that much of the planet has fared better than our little corner. To believe is a powerful thing. It can keep you from despair; it can offer you salvation. *Belief* is sometimes all you have, your faith. I lost it once…

Additional Resources:

www.mikepoeltl.com- official website for the series

More books by Michael Poeltl

Rebirth (Book two of The Judas Syndrome)
Revelation (Book three of The Judas Syndrome)
Her Past's Present
Available on Amazon

About the author

Website: www.mikepoeltl.com
Twitter: @mpoeltlauthor
Facebook: Michael.Poeltl.author
Amazon Author Page: Michael Poeltl Amazon

www.ingramcontent.com/pod-product-compliance
Lightning Source LLC
Chambersburg PA
CBHW032006240626
47153CB00003B/1148